A Year Out

Beverley Coghlan

PublishAmerica

PublishAmerica
Baltimore

First printing

ISBN: 1-4137-7043-6
PUBLISHED BY PUBLISHAMERICA, LLLP
www.publishamerica.com
Baltimore

Printed in the United States of America

This book is dedicated to my most precious
daughter Sarah Jane.

A Year Out

1

---❈---

In Training

2nd March 2003
"This will be your home for the next six months," said Granville,
opening the door of the vehicle. "Our freedom from the tyranny of
labour!" he added with a flourish.
I climbed determinedly into the camper-van, looking around at
the compact interior.
*I must be off the wall…stark raving mad to agree to this. But
I can't back out now.*
I am not a natural camper. It was Granville's dream to have an
extended holiday travelling around on wheels. The idea definitely did
not come from me! When we first married in 1990, he spoke of his
longing to buy a caravan or camper and to travel the world. Right
now I desperately need a break. If this is to be the only way out….I
must try it. (Secretly, I thought that if I longed for a hot bath and soak,
I could book into a hotel or bed and breakfast).
Why do I need to get away? For the past seven years I have
worked exhaustingly hard at developing my career in the UK, and
previously I had been immersed in this demanding career since the
late 1970's. It has not been easy. I have had enough, and Granville
is delighted that I have finally agreed to escape.
How will I cope without the stress? Will I miss the buzz of the

business-drug I have lived with for the past thirty years? Will the cold turkey be too painful? How difficult will it be to leave behind the addictive, stress-fuelled world of goals, targets and deadlines? I am going to take the chance. After all, it will only be for a few months.

With some relief, I can pack away the corporate uniform of smart dark trouser suits, comfortable Van Dal shoes, the ever- present, ever-buzzing mobile phone, briefcase and all the other tools of the trade that essentially accompany the promotion of houses to expatriates in the home counties of England. In this new life, my accessories will be a laptop to record my diary; books I have wanted to read for years; watercolour materials and sketch-block. I'll need pullovers, denims, cords and track suits, and a serious parka…and where do I find a really waterproof raincoat? Take-off is two weeks away!

The Sunday after we made the decision to take a Sabbatical, we decide to combine our verbal planning with getting fit. Most evenings I fall in the door having been at the office for at least ten hours and am so exhausted that we rarely have time to discuss anything important. Ever since we married thirteen years ago, Granville (bless him) and I have lived a sort of role reversal. He cooks and shops (both of which he does with much passion!). My generous waistline bares testimony. He keeps house while I have the full-time anchor job. And today the get-fit training begins.

"It's all in the planning," said Granville, compass in hand as we set off from the National Trust Car Park at Runnymead (outside Windsor, Berkshire), a few miles from our home. Our first ramble will take us through a pretty meadow where, in 1215, King John sealed the Magna Charta, and up the gentle hillside to the Air Force Memorial. Then the homeward route…down the hill to the American Bar Association Memorial and John F. Kennedy Memorial and, finally, back along the river to a cup of tea, scones and jam (and yes…cream too) at the little National Trust restaurant.

But the reality is a different tale! The pretty meadow quickly gives way to mushy mud which sticks to our walking shoes, and I find within a few minutes I am at least three inches taller. We start the ascent of the 'gentle' hillside through the bare trees, which were beginning to show signs of life, and realize that it's not only muddy in the valley: the climb up was of the 'one step forward and slip-and-slide back two' variety. After struggling for forty-five minutes, the gentle hillside felt like Kilimanjaro.

Unfortunately, we were too puffed to discuss our future plans. Granville was doing much better than I was, but even so, his eyes were bulging a little from exertion, and he was not saying much, which was amazing for him. I have always said that when he stops talking I know he is asleep (or dead).

An hour and a half later, we reached the top. The magnificent Air Force Memorial is a tribute to thousands of British and Allied air force men and women who lost their lives in the Second World War. The solid, plain building is rather like the towers of the early airport buildings constructed in the thirties and forties in South Africa, where I lived until moving to the UK in 1996.

Overlooking the valley…the view was wonderful, far-reaching from left to right. Below us lay the towns of Egham, Thorpe and Windsor. To the right we could see Heathrow Airport with plane after plane lifting off and landing every few seconds. None of these dead airmen could have known that their memorial would be silent witness to jets and planes and supersonic wonders like Concorde. (Now sadly withdrawn from service; it was such magnificent sight).

After an hour, we had recovered our breath and were congratulating ourselves on having survived the long haul up the hill.

"It should be much easier, going down," I said rather misguidedly.

It's a slippery descent. For brevity, I will say that we ran down the hill: not by choice. For most of it, we couldn't have stopped if we'd wanted to. The initial idea was to get my body used to walking and in training for the more physically active outdoor days ahead. Already I feel as if I have shaken up parts of me I did not know existed.

My friends and family would be surprised to see me deliberately expend so much energy. The office girls always joked that I would catch a taxi to Boots (across the road) and to my car—if it is parked more than 100 metres away—but this is a little unfair. I have been selling houses since 1978, and that longevity speaks volumes for my resilience and energy: to last that long in the property industry, one needs the optimism and agility of a happy puppy. I do not mind exercise. I have been known to run…well…ok…walk fast… provided there is purpose. So our inaugural hike has given me a foretaste of what lies ahead. The fact that our intention was to discuss the result of Granville's investigations into buying a camper and what we were going to do with the house, my job and other important issues, was temporarily forgotten. Oh well, time enough.

I should have been paralysed today—after yesterday's long hike—but I wasn't. I have just realized why. This Monday was typical of my normal daily business activities as a relocation agent. I have shown sales applicants two houses in Wentworth Private Estate (arguably one of the best private estates in Berkshire or even in the UK…so the blurb goes). Both houses are over ten thousand square feet in size, excluding their gardens. As I was climbing floor three to show the au pair/granny flat, it suddenly dawned; I climb and walk all day! I just don't know I am doing the exercise thing. But it's what I do!

The first property we visited this morning had a large garden 'of over two acres' in extent. The enthusiastic owner accompanied the tour, pointing out the 'important' features of his estate—fruit trees, just visible daffodils, large magnolia that always had a spectacular flowering in April (I couldn't see a bud), special authentic York stone flagstones and so on. He also insisted that we inspect the lovely rhododendrons (not in flower yet) that formed a hedge around the entire perimeter of the property. When we returned to the house, he insisted on showing my African-American clients, Mr and Mrs Jones, the bulging photo album of what the garden would look like in spring and summer, what the house looked like before they added the recreation wing, and finally, their last Christmas party with the entire family from Holland.

Mr and Mrs Jones smiled graciously whilst, with superb dexterity, they started walking backwards. I think they have been house-hunting for some time! To their credit, they were still smiling (a little warily) when the vendor rushed out to their car as they were backing out of the drive to ask if they had seen the new gazebo and conservatory plans. Noticing the panic beginning to show in their eyes, I intervened and said I knew that Mr and Mrs Jones had a luncheon appointment and really need to get away. The look of love and gratitude they beamed at me was confirmation that we were on the same wavelength.

I wonder if vendors know how off-putting it can be when they take over from the agent and pedantically point out the attributes in detail to buyers. It smacks of desperation and can ruin what could be a successful viewing. I know that estate agents are as favoured as 'a ham sandwich in a synagogue', but there are two sides to the story: some sellers (and also some buyers or house-hunters) can be exhausting.

Anyhow, back to my daily exercise. I am already in training—but now more consciously. I walk briskly as I go about the task of securing the sale or letting of just one more house (if I am lucky two) before I set off on the great trek. Mr and Mrs Jones will not be one of my successes: they have decided to continue to rent a home in Egham (near the American School) for the duration of the five year contract Mr Jones has with an oil company.

4th March

Today I am 53. It's dawning on me that we are taking a huge step. No income for a year. At our age, is this a stupid risk? Granville and I know that we're entering a new phase of our lives. I have to get away from the pressures of real estate for a while.

After the dreadful events of 9/11 there was a radical change in the house-buying market, especially around Ascot, Berkshire, with its large international and American population. In the past six months, I have found the pressure getting to me. There was a clear downturn in the property industry, which, up to then, had been frantic (with appreciation in some areas as high as 140%) during an eighteen month period. I didn't mind working hard when we were successfully tying up deals, but in the last few months, it just wasn't happening—the phrase 'farting against thunder' comes to mind. I was praying for a reprieve. Granville wanted peace and quietness from his daily routine to finish a book…any one of the three he was writing simultaneously! Experiences and education have equipped him to complete one or all of these books, but he needs the time.

Perhaps this was the time for serious change.

One Sunday in early February, we were discussing our lives…and how much we wanted to break away.

"Why don't we throw in the whole lot, pack in our jobs, buy a camper-van and just travel for a year or so? We will come back broke, but what the heck!" I heard myself saying.

Granville looked at me, obviously shocked to hear this suggestion from my lips.

"Yes! Yes! Yes!" he said, alive with joy.

On the evening of my birthday, we celebrate with our three boys: Gregory at twenty-six (Granville's son), Allan at twenty-four (my son), Patrick at twenty-three (Granville's son) and Patty, Gregory's girlfriend. She is a lovely 'peaches and cream' English girl, delicate and sensitive. I have to tread carefully—she is still not used to my South African directness.

We eat plate-loads of pasta at our local Italian restaurant, drink red wine and share our plans with the family. We tell them about our idea to buy a camper-van and head off for a few months to restore the brain cells. We do not need to explain that I have burnt out after working in the property industry without a break for many years nor that their father has similarly spent his life occupied in one way or another. Our family toasts the new venture. It is so great to know that the boys are really supportive, enthusiastic and happy for us. I thought they might have tried to get us certified!

It gives us joy to see them happy in their own lives—each so very different but strong and resilient. They have survived many changes in the post-apartheid South Africa: sadness as dozens of their friends moved out of the country, tough times as our real estate business suffered the ill-effects of a bad market, the devastating loss of their sister at twenty-one years in December 1995, and latterly, our decision to move to a new country.

5th March
The camper-van has arrived. It looks like an impatient monster blocking the driveway, dwarfing the cars. Granville washed and cleaned it lovingly, inside and out, scrubbing the fat tyres with my kitchen brush. Later, he gently dabbed and painted its scratches and bruises as if it were a little child.

I happily leave the packing, fitting, fixing and all the preparations to Granville. He is the master planner, and each holiday or trip we have taken in the past (no matter how short) was organised with military precision. Granville has sixty-eight years under his belt (a bit tight now) and has worked hard for most it. After a spell in the army, he studied and became a teacher at a private, family-owned school before becoming headmaster when his father retired.

At about forty-five years of age, Granville arrived in South Africa with wife number two and two little children, where he joined a large international company...but he was also nursing a failing second marriage. It was only a matter of time before he once again found himself single, but this time with his young boys.

My relationship with Granville began when I sold him a house. Determined now to focus on his children and on being a dad, he had chosen to make a new career for himself as a free lance writer—free from the demands of the large organisation that had taken him away from home so much. Five weeks after our first date, I phoned my mom and dad (a farmer-preacher) to say I was getting married. You can imagine my dad's consternation when I told him that my beloved was out of work, not a professing Christian, and had two boisterous boys. My precious family were especially troubled when I couldn't spell his surname!

"You are rushing into this," my worried dad warned. "He's after your money."

And here we are in England thirteen years later. Much has happened since our marriage in 1990, and we are really tired. The year we married, we bought a property business and put together two sets of kids: mine—Lucy and Allan, and Granville's two boys—Gregory and Patrick. The first few years of our marriage were busy, happy, at times crazy.

Business was excellent. Property was booming after the euphoria following the fall of apartheid: the Group Areas Act had been rescinded. (This was the sick law in the Apartheid era where people were prevented from living where they wanted—they had to reside in the area set aside for their racial group). Nelson Mandela was elected president of South Africa in 1994, and there were huge changes in political and day-to-day happenings all around us. We were able to enjoy an affluent lifestyle: a large home, servants, holidays overseas, a caravan, boat and other luxuries.

Our children were growing up, becoming people with a voice and strong opinions. Many family battles were fought in those years. Granville and I had very different ways of discipline and general childrearing. I thought he was too soft…he thought I was far too tough. My philosophy was 'spare the rod and spoil the child' whereas Granville held strong Dr Spock beliefs that gave children the freedom to express themselves. As an ex-headmaster, he spent a lot of time explaining and reasoning. I didn't! We had decided when the families came together that he would take care of the discipline of his boys, and I would sort out Lucy and Allan when they stepped out of line.

One incidence still makes me laugh. Allan and Patrick, then thirteen and eleven respectively, had vandalised an office building under construction by shooting out newly fitted strip lights with their pellet guns. We lived in a small town, and I was soon informed of the misdeed by the exasperated Zulu watchman. When confronted, the boys readily admitted guilt, and I gave Allan a good hiding and sent him to his room to repent. I told Patrick to wait for his dad to 'sort him out'.

"Please, Anne…can't you give me a hiding? I couldn't stand another one of Dad's long lectures," Patrick begged, mockingly falling down on his knees. They were wonderful times.

In one awful year—1995 (I think everyone has at least one particular 'annus horriblis', even Her Majesty the Queen of England)—several things happened to change the course of our lives. Firstly, as the year began, the property market plummeted. Hundreds of white South Africans were leaving the country; they called it the 'chicken run.'

In April, Granville had a massive stroke. He was seriously ill for months afterwards, and the prognosis was that if he survived at all, he would have a reduced functioning of sight and mobility. There was a chance if he had an operation to remove a clot from his carotid artery, but none of the surgeons would operate on him. They considered the risk too high and that he would stroke again during the operation when the unstable clots became dislodged. Several weeks after the episode, a friend of a friend told me of a brilliant vascular surgeon: an Indian returning to South Africa after having spent years in Ireland as a political refugee. He offered to operate but warned me that Granville had less than a 30% chance of surviving the operation. We held a family conference (Granville was not capable of making any decisions at this time) and decided to go ahead with the operation. Our logic was that in his present state, he had such a poor quality of life that he couldn't see properly or even walk unaided. We were also told that one supply of blood to his brain was totally blocked, and the other could well close within weeks. By this time, Granville had accepted the Lord as Saviour, and he prayed with strong faith and simple trust in Jesus that he would pull through. The operation was an amazing success. He regained consciousness asking (actually…demanding) a cup of tea, and he went from strength to strength, recovering fully within a few months.

My darling granny (mum's mum) departed this life in July (she was 94). At the end of the year, our much loved gardener who lived in a cottage (the kia) at the bottom of our garden died in a hit-and-run accident. But the greatest catalyst for change in our lives happened in December of that year, when my daughter Lucy was killed. She had just had her twenty-first birthday. It was a very sad Christmas.

By the beginning of the next year, the two older boys had finished high school and were heading for work or university. Patrick was absorbed by the yachting and deep sea diving scene. Lucy's death had a huge impact on their lives as well as on ours, of course, in the personal, social and business spheres. I threw myself into our property business in an effort to ignore (just for a few hours) the awfulness of what had happened and the ever present pain, but escape was futile. In my home town (there were hundreds of people at her funeral), I couldn't turn around without someone with sad eyes, saying, "How are you? Is it getting easier?" or even more annoyingly, "Look at the positive side, you still have the boys?"

I know they meant well, but most people have no idea of how to handle the grieving, especially if they have not suffered the loss of someone close them. Either they ignore the whole thing and avoid all mention of the deceased or go all mournful the moment you come onto the horizon like they are actors in the play doing the 'sad, look sad' bit. We found some of our dearest dinner-party friends started to avoid us, and there was an awkwardness that had not been there previously.

One day over lunch at a shopping centre in Westville near Durban, Granville and I were discussing our future. Should we sell the business and move to another area? Should we go on an extended holiday break (God knows we needed one)?

"What about going overseas to England? I need the break, and I will do a bit of a reconnaissance when I am there," I voiced, watching him carefully.

I saw relief on his face, but he replied, "You will never get a job, and the cold will kill you! But why not take Allan with you and have a three week holiday? The change will do you good."

Leaving Granville to 'man the shop' in South Africa, I arrived in London in early 1996 with my son. It was freezing cold. My thin coat was no protection from the icy wind. In KwaZulu Natal, we hardly ever had temperatures below 12 degrees centigrade, and I had never visited the UK in winter before. The prices in the shops were exorbitant when converted into Rand (the South African currency), but a sweet little shop assistant in The House of Fraser in Guildford High Street, Surrey, noticing my distress, told me about charity shops. Wonderful things, charity shops! I found a really serious winter coat for just seven pounds and a cashmere scarf for two pounds fifty. Allan found a leather bomber jacket for five pounds.

Our plans were sketchy. Basically, we wanted to travel around the south of England to see what business opportunities there were within the Real Estate industry; also to have a holiday. Allan was very close to his big sister, and her death had affected him massively, so he was grateful to accompany me. Muffled up with scarves, gloves and charity shop coats, we did all the tourist kind of things…it was wonderful to unwind in this strange frosty place.

I visited friends I hadn't seen for years, enjoying long 'catch up' chats. One Danish friend I had worked with in South Africa during the '80s, Tom Hegel, had opened an exclusive property company in London. More recently, he had expanded and now had a branch of his business, Global Real Estates, in Ascot, Berkshire, within commuting distance of several international schools. It was interesting to compare notes. We had both trained in South Africa under the doyen of property in our area.

I visited several estate agents in and around London with a view to relocating and finding work in the industry. This was quite an experience. Going from office to office, I was amazed how few agents would stand up to greet me! I had called to enquire about the estate agency business and not to buy or sell a house, but what if I had been an applicant with a lot of money to spend? I was shocked by their attitude and general demeanour.

My confusion increased when I discovered that in England, there was no mandatory or compulsory qualification before one could operate as an estate agent! No licence, no fidelity certificate, no indemnity insurance, no legal or educational requirements! How interesting!

I assumed that the levels of schooling and entry-level qualifications required for any industry would be superior to that of South Africa. I reasoned that the average school-leaver is considered sufficiently *au fait* with common law and property law, language and selling skills as to make any further certificate unnecessary. How wrong could I be? It appeared that the residential sales agencies were male dominated and, last but not least, to my horror, I found there was no multi-listing. Anyhow, I was still excited about getting into the industry. I was sure that I could learn many first-world business skills, sophisticated methods of marketing and property promotion. Wow! Once I got involved in the industry in England, I soon found that nothing could be further from the reality!

Allan and I went down to the coastal areas near Eastbourne that were once Granville's home ground. The business scene was scary, but we enjoyed the cute seaside towns, strange pebble beaches and much lower cost of living. We also discovered wonderful fish-and-chips…and the Edinburgh Wool Shops, where I stocked up on more woolly things to keep us warm.

While we were on the coast, I contacted my London friend, Tom Hegel, to thank him and his wife for their hospitality and to tell him that we were settled on the coast for a few weeks. Out of the blue, he offered me a job. He wanted me to start a relocation and property acquisition division for the company using methods that Danish and other expatriates would find user-friendly. They say that fools rush in…and that is just what I did. Excited with the new challenge, I phoned Granville, who was equally delighted. He said he had been praying that I would get a job offer; in the short time I had been away, the market had worsened. He said that he would pack up the house and close the business.

"Just can't wait to join you!" he said, adding, "The pommies are different, so it is *not* going to be easy for you. The business world of England will be vastly different from your friendly small-town experience in Kwa Zulu Natal."

Had I known then just how different it would be, I might not have tackled the enterprise with such joyful anticipation.

Allan was supportive of our move to England and remained with me. All we could afford in the way of housing was a small flat in

Chertsey that was the same size in total as my bedroom in South Africa. I tried to dissuade Granville from bringing the contents of our seven bedroom house, which filled eighty-three tea boxes of small goods and a huge container. When he arrived a few months later, the truth dawned, and he realized that we would have to change our lifestyle considerably to survive.

I started working from a small Ascot office in July 1996. My first task was to draw up a basic business plan for relocation and property searches, read as much as I could about the legal process, and institute rules and method of promotion, etc. Then I was ready to launch into the operation with enthusiasm.

Unexpectedly, it was my naivety that opened some doors for me, but generally it was difficult to break into that closed shop. For example, I had no idea that cold canvassing was 'not done' (especially in the prime areas) and that contacting a vendor who had a board displayed outside his house was considered 'touting'. Nevertheless, I enjoyed the therapy of being totally absorbed and also finding refuge in anonymity. In England, few people knew about Lucy. So, being in England working at a project was salvation in itself. I was too busy to weep, and there weren't the constant reminders. Anyhow, I have always believed *my* grief is *my* package. I made a conscious effort to leave my bundle of problems outside the door of my office and only allow myself to pick it up when I went home. No one else deserves my sadness. It's easier to forget when one is five thousand miles from home.

The process of purchasing or renting a home here in England is hugely different from buying a home in South Africa or in America. Here, the entire system and procedure is fraught with pitfalls and problems. I soon discovered that it was a nerve-wracking process that started with a verbal agreement between the buyer and seller, but there was (and still is) no enforceable contact at the outset of the sale. For the first time in my life, I learned the term 'gazumping'. This seems to be a word peculiar to the English real estate sales scene. To explain: A buyer can proceed towards his purchase (often at considerable expense) only to have the seller change his or her mind (often at the last minute) and accept a better offer. They buyer would be gazumped from the sale! Nothing in the law exists to stop this, and the buyer has no recourse to recover the costs already incurred. Most people in England find it is a ghastly time in their lives when they move home. I am going to jump off my hobby-horse right now, or this will dominate my story! I could write tomes about the unique property purchasing system in England.

By early 1997, the real estate industry, particularly in the South of England, was madly busy. Ascot—an easy commute for the corporate commuter to London—was popular and buzzing. I was really grateful to have a rewarding venture to chew into. The hard work was rewarded with good success, and my friend (now my boss) opened two other branches, one in Guildford, Surrey, and another not far from the Ascot office in Virginia Water. Our relocation and property acquisition division became highly respected.

Looking back over the past seven years, Granville, Allan and I have worked long hours and learnt some hard lessons. (Granville's boys too have had similar experiences—they followed us over to the UK in 2001), the most important being that it was impossible to duplicate the lifestyle we left behind: servants, large house, boat, and luxurious holidays. It was essential to accept the changes in our way of life and adapt accordingly.

In the workplace or socially in our adopted country, few people were particularly interested in what we had, did or were during our past life 'at home'. We arrived with very little money when converted into pounds. The exchange rate from the South African Rand (currency) was (still is) pitiful, so we had to start all over again. In late 1997, we bought a little flat in a very good area, sold it for a whole lot more than we had paid for it, and then we bought another property. We have improved our present home too, when we could find the time and money. The property business was excellent for the first five years, and Granville worked at developing a small training school as well as continue with his writing.

7th March

Breaking the news to my boss was not easy. I took him to lunch at a local French restaurant. After several glasses of wine and a superb meal, I told him of my impending travel plans and my need to get away.

"Whaaaaaaaaaaaat! You're kidding!" he yelled over his cappuccino.

"You know that the Berkshire and Surrey offices are a madhouse during the summer when we start the busy season with all the European and American families coming over. You are coming back...aren't you...you're my anchor!" he shouted.

"You can't leave me!" he added plaintively. People in the restaurant were looking at us as I tried to pacify him.

"Yes, of course, Tom, I'll be back. I just need a break." But there wasn't much enthusiasm or certainty in my voice.

That evening when Granville and I walked by the river, I told him of my boss's reaction. I don't think he heard too much of what I was saying. He was too busy mentally packing and planning our trip.

9th March

Already the attitudes of my colleagues at work are changing. They don't believe I am coming back after our sabbatical. They think I have another job lined up, or it has even been suggested that I am starting my own business! We have worked together for seven years now, and I know how much I shall miss them. We have shared a whole lot of fun—had some good, some bad and some mad times. *Panic...there is so much to do before I go!*

I need to train someone to do my job and put in place systems that will make it possible for someone else to pick up the ball and run with it, although the property industry at the moment is not exactly buoyant, so there will not be too much to run with!

The pending war (Blair and Bush, the bosom buddies, want to knock out Saddam Hussein even though it is against the United Nations vote) is strongly in the news. Granville, on one of our evening walks, was going on and on about the pending war in Iraq and how the British Labour party were making a mess of the country. I really laughed when he threw in the statement, "Going to war is one of those *bad decisions* that Tony Blair and Labour are getting better and better at making."

Granville blames everything that goes wrong (including his ingrown toenails) on 'President Blair'. No matter one's political opinions, this situation has got everyone in the property business really twitchy. Global Real Estates aim for the top end of the market, mainly promoting properties in excess of £500,000 to wealthy private and some large corporate clients. Since the end of 2001, when the twin towers were so horrifically and tragically targeted (and fell, following the act of monumental madness), the buying power in this sector has been drastically reduced. There followed a general world-wide slowdown in the economy: stock markets plummeted in most Western countries, and the international business scene was very nervous. Property sales and relocations were a mirror of these reactions.

I don't think we will have appreciable growth in the next few months in fact. Not for quite a while. So this is the right time to take a break.

11th March

This evening, Granville and I talk about how different our days will be when we are away. He has bought a really powerful laptop for writing his books, with every facility. 'All the whistles and bows', my mom would have said. I just wanted to keep a diary, so I bought a cheap laptop that was on on special!

We try to collate our ideas and get things in order for our absence from home. There are insurance and banking matters to sort out, we need to arrange for key holders for our house, and most importantly, we need to find a foster home for our cat, Pussy Willow.

Granville spends most of his time getting the camper as comfortable and homelike as possible. He has visited the camper-company shop so many times, I think they must grit their teeth when they see his car coming around the corner. He is so excited and in hamster-mode. There are bundles of clothes, boxes of food and lots of other bags of stuff scattered all over the house, which he assures me will fit perfectly into the cupboards and storage compartments of the camper.

"Is it *that* big?" I asked.

12th March

We have just returned home after taking Pussy Willow to her foster home. I mentioned to a newly arrived Canadian friend last evening that I would need a temporary home for our cat. She said that her youngest son would be delighted to look after kitty while we were away. He, the son aged eight, loved cats and missed having animals since they moved to the UK. His mom felt that having a pet might be just what he needed.

Pussy Willow travelled well in her cat-basket and, provided she could hear our voices, she was quiet and relaxed. If we stopped talking for a while, she gave a pathetic meow just to check that all was fine.

*I am so relieved to find someone who wants to look after her.
I would have hated to put her in a cattery.*

We needn't have worried. It was love at first sight. The young kitty-minder is a bookish chap, and I know they will get on fabulously. The next few days will be a trial period: we will have time to make alternative arrangements if they are not compatible. We warn the family that our kitty is lovely, but she comes with some baggage. No, we do not mean the blankets, food, special bowl, scratching post, flea control drops (very, very important…she is allergic to flea bites), cat cage, etc. We warn the family that Pussy Willow is an early riser—a furry alarm clock. She taps you on the head at 5.30 a.m. (on the nail) for her breakfast. If you ignore her, she sometimes resorts to violence, and the scars on top of Granville's bald head are proof that she knows how to get the message across. This has not been too much of a problem for us because I get up early most mornings anyhow. Apart from this strange behaviour, kitty is sweet, loving, clean and an absolute joy. Our guests and visitors love her—she is very sociable and always greets anyone who calls.

That night, I feel that there is something missing from the bottom of the bed where she usually sleeps. I woke at 5.30 a.m., but it was too early to phone them, so I wait until 9.00 a.m. to see how they survived. A very sleepy voice answered the phone.

"It wasn't too bad except Pussy Willow followed mummy to the loo in the middle of the night, and she was yowling at about 5.30, jumping from bed to bed trying to wake someone up."

To their credit, they ignored her until 7 a.m. Apparently, it took much resolve and determination to ignore the caterwauling and antics. I feel confident that Pussy Willow will either settle to later feeding times within a few days, or someone will be enjoying the sunrise on a regular basis!

With only a few days left at the office, I was frantically busy setting up easy-to-follow instructions for Susan and the other girls, nurturing the sales-in-progress to prepare for exchange or conclusion. My boss had decided not to replace me, but they were going to bring in part-time staff if they could not cope. He also phoned several times, uncharacteristically picking away at petty things. Then the senior accountant had the audacity to e-mail me. "My eagle eye has noticed that you took an extra two days after your conference in Hong Kong. I know it was a business trip, but you have not put in a holiday requisition form. And I think you made some calls to Spain from your hotel. Were these personal? And regarding petty cash, I noticed there were several items on the bill from Sainsbury's that could be for your home use?"

"Yes, some of them could be…" I replied as soon as I saw the e-mail, "…but they weren't! Don't you remember that we had a function last month and that is why we bought two dozen paper napkins and some wineglasses? Regarding the phone calls: we have clients in Spain and all over the world for that matter…so feel free to check the numbers!" I raged on, banging the keyboard. "By the way, where was your eagle eye when I put in an average of seventy-two hours work per week over the past six years and when I paid for client coffees or lunches (not charging them to my expense account)? Your eagle eyes must have been shut when I paid for office necessities that I should have charged to petty cash! I have never short-changed the company, and I certainly am not starting now!" I finished snottily.

The penny pinching and suspicious attitude was unnecessary, and it really grated me.

I certainly need this Sabbatical.

13th March
As part of our financial planning, we know it will be easier if we can find tenants to occupy our home while we are away. It will pay

the costs and overheads and enable us to travel for longer. We have registered our property with two agencies to find us a tenant. To date, the letting agents have brought a strange assortment of potential applicants: From bored Americans (exasperated that their letting budget would not stretch to a large family home complete with pool and acre of land) to a single mum with three small children (and no visible means of support) to some Scandinavians who love the light modern interior but needed more space, and even several families from 'up north'. During a viewing, I overhear an agent in her Home Counties accent telling someone who has just arrived from Edinburgh,

"You don't get much for your money in Berkshire."

After each viewing by a potential tenant, Granville and I discuss our feelings regarding the applicant (although having been in the industry for many years, it is just what I have always told my clients *not* to do). Many times I have advised my clients and homeowners, "Don't take it *personally* if they don't like your house or you don't like them. They are just buying/renting your home—you don't have to fall in *love* with them."

Nevertheless, we continue to assess each applicant with the 'Would we like them living in our home?' attitude!

One chap made an offer that we rejected. He was visiting the UK for three months, bringing a nanny to look after his nine year old son. They were also 'getting a rescued puppy to amuse the boy'. They planned to return the dog to the dog's home before returning home! When we refused the offer, the letting agent thought we were dog/puppy/animal haters and sent me few caustic e-mails. One poem was about animals being God's precious creatures and how we should treasure them. It took a whole lot of control to explain delicately that *we* were, in fact, dog lovers and felt that anyone who 'borrows' a puppy to give back after a few months cannot *possibly* care much for the animal.

So our home is still not yet rented out. We are just going to lock up and head off on our vacation, leaving keys with the boys, the estate agents and our kind neighbours.

14th March

Friday! It's my last day at the office before we head off. I wake early to have a short power walk around the estate where we live. My fitness training programme has become reduced to this daily walk and my estate agency activities! The past few days have been harrowing. I tried to leave everything easily accessible in the Relocation and Acquisitions department so that whoever was brought in to fill the gap whilst I was away would be able to find and access any information she/he might require.

At lunch time, I brought in Chinese food for everyone and am really glad that I did. The staff from the other offices also came to say goodbye. As we stood sharing some of the crazy things that had happened to us as agents, it confirmed my belief that we always see the real side of our colleagues only when they are relaxed and informal, just as we see the true character of our clients when we visit their properties. Viewing their homes is looking into their hearts and lives. We know when clients are selling or letting because they are getting divorced (one side of the double bed is vacant of personal objects: a giveaway!), if they have lost their husband/wife (they are very sad and it's hard not to get involved), and if they are leaving for bigger and better (we are usually proudly told at the outset). "We're moving, we need more space. We are 'trading up'."

Over the lunch, we shared some of our stories and 'was my face red' moments…so many strange tales to tell of our times in the property industry. I suggested we collate the stories and write a book!

I thought Helena (manager from Guildford office) was going to choke on her *chicken foo yung* when I related the following contribution:

"I had a client, Mr Cox, who popped in to the office to see me. I was on the phone at the time and, noticing him waiting for me, said without thinking, 'I will be with you in a moment, Mr Dick'. I continued with the phone call 'til a few seconds later I realised my mistake. I don't recall ending the conversation, but there was no way to explain that error. I think Mr Cox noticed and kindly ignored my Freudian slip."

Another story they seemed to find amusing:

"I was showing a house to applicants, and the owner worked far away from home. He was seldom there except on weekends. He had given us a key, and as I opened the door to the super home, I had a fleeting thought that it looked more 'lived in' than usual but that most likely it was just my imagination. When my clients (a family consisting of mum, dad and two teenage children) and I reached the master en-suite bathroom, I flung the door open, and there was Mr X, sitting on the loo. I froze for a few seconds then backed into my clients, muttering apologies. We only started laughing once we got back into my car. The kids thought it was a show worth remembering and are probably still 'dining out' on this story ten years on. When I phoned to apologise, the seller of the house was not at all put out!

'My dear' he said, 'I was going to stand up and shake your hand, but I knew you would be even more embarrassed, and with your fair skin, I thought you could have done yourself some damage'."

As I prepare to leave the posh office this afternoon, I am a little apprehensive. Having worked virtually non-stop (except to produce babies) for the past thirty years, I am not sure how it will be not to have a totally structured day. We will soon find out! Susan is really worried. We have worked together happily for the past six years. She is understandably nervous.

"Is the company folding?" she asked me privately.

Susan is our office Mrs Malaprop. One of the funny stories that came out of her malapropisms was when I happened to be passing the kitchen at the office and found her choking on a dry bread roll. I saw her in distress and administered the Heimlich manoeuvre. When the other staff returned from lunch, I heard her telling them, "Anne saved my life! I was dying and choking, and she did the 'hind leg' manoeuvre on me!"

With good wishes and a sweet gift of Jo Malone travel cosmetics from the girls, we say our goodbyes. I feel like I have been put out of the playpen and hope I can pick up and carry on when the need arises. My boss is sulking and doesn't even say goodbye. My company car has gone back to the dealer, and Granville picks me up in his little banger. It's a bit strange not to be in the big Mercedes automatic, and it comes to me that if there is anything about the job I may miss it could be the car.

This evening, Lois (South African girl friend) brings us a lovely meal so that we can continue packing to get off early tomorrow. The evening was special. It was one of those impromptu happenings that don't come often. The boys also came to say goodbye. We laughed about all sorts of stupid things. They were so genuine and loving in their good wishes for us. They have seen us slog away for years—they know we need this break.

I look around our cosy lounge this goodbye evening and at the boys. Gregory, who became the eldest when Lucy was killed, is smart, always immaculate and turn-heads good looking. His academic achievements outshine all his siblings' efforts, and they respect his qualifications without envy. Once they may have, but I think rivalry and pettiness died a while ago. Gregory is returning to South Africa to further his Veterinary Medicine studies. I know that if he puts his mind to it, he will achieve the best results.

On the day he arrived here in England after finishing his basic degree in South Africa, our young neighbour Patty came to welcome him. It was love at first flutter, and they have been inseparable ever since. I wonder if she will join him in South Africa. Somehow I think it is a hard place, tough and at times cruel. I am not sure if she has got what it takes to survive in that environment. I must not interfere; she may love it. She may be stronger than she appears.

Allan has recently embraced the Christian faith and found much joy in reading and studying God's word. He is very involved with the Alpha Christian Movement that started at Holy Trinity, Brompton in London and is getting baptised (full immersion) on the 11th May. I remember what a little shit he was in his teenage years! We had many sleepless nights while he smoked dagga (marijuana), stabbed himself with drugs and did the mad 'arty' thing. I finally threw him out, along with all the waifs and strays he had collected, when they ignored the warnings we gave them to clean up their act. At the time, there were seven guys living in the bed-sit which was attached to our home. They were living like pigs, smoking dagga and taking hard drugs. Finally the 'damage-the-brain' music and smell of dagga got to me, and I put all their clothes, bedding and other stuff into a whole lot of black rubbish bags, dumped them in the driveway and relocated the whole gang to the country, where I had found them a little tumble-down cottage. God knows what went on there. Lucy was very protective of her brother and said, "Mums, you're being horrible to Bubs. It's only a stage."

I know that for a fact she visited them and took food parcels and clean clothes (I think she sneaked their washing into our laundry!).

After Lucy died, Allan and I were packing up her room, putting her clothes into bundles to give to charity, and he said, "You know, Mom, I never had an ugly fight with Lucy…not ever. She was always so kind; the kindest person in the whole world."

He loved her, and they were very close—closer than most brothers and sisters usually are. He held her hand while she was dying. Lucy had just turned twenty-one, and the accident that killed her is still a mystery.

Patrick is my step-son, but I often forget he is not my blood son. Several times have people said that he looks like me. We were waiting at the doctor's surgery just after I married Granville when the nurse turned to him and said, "You must be Anne's son…you look just like her."

Patrick was nine when Granville and I were married, and I could write a few volumes on all the drama that he created. He is, and in those mad years was, the most loving, sensitive, highly intelligent and generous child. But in his growing years, when his hormones were raging and he was 'finding himself', he was a nightmare for teacher, parents, or anyone in authority. At thirteen, he was six-foot-four-inches tall and was built like a tank. He played rugby, loved to surf and party, and was always on the go. If there wasn't enough excitement, he could be relied on to make it happen! There were parties and fights and drama of all kinds—never a dull moment. He ran away from home regularly. His father despairingly used to leave Lucy and I to hunt for him. Sometimes we found him on Durban beachfront, camping wild in the bush or sleeping over with a friend. He was rebellious and difficult.

A few months after Lucy died (he was fifteen), he pulled out of school of his own volition and said he was never going back. He got a job in a bar (he was bar manager within a few months: he is *exceptionally* bright), and when he had saved enough money, he took a sailing and navigation course at the Royal Yacht club. He passed brilliantly. Then, gathering together a small backpack and telling us not to worry, he boarded a yacht in Durban and went sailing around the world. I have corns on my knees from praying for him. Since then, he has added to his yachting experiences and qualifications by doing lifesaving and deep sea diving to instructor and rescue level. He is without doubt one of the sharpest minds I have ever come across. He has a photographic memory. He now lives nearby and has recently joined the corporate world in a company aligned to the sailing industry. It'll be interesting to see where life takes him. Or, more accurately, where he takes life!

By the way…kitty is fine. She has settled well and is relaxed and happy. She breakfasts at 7.30 a.m.

I must find out how they achieved that!

2

We're Off!

15th March

It feels really strange to be driving in such a huge vehicle. As we set off on our inaugural trip, Granville carefully navigates around the poles, barriers and overhanging branches. I feel that everyone in the road is watching our departure.

Cooden Beach, East Sussex was our first overnight stop. As a child, Granville played on this strange little beach just outside Bexhill-on-sea. He was born a few miles away in Little Common. It is familiar territory, but it's going to take me a while to get used to our strange new 'shell'.

We found firm pebbles upon which to park the van. The wind was howling and freezing cold. Not surprisingly, there were no other cars or vehicles. Granville produced a delicious sausage and mash meal with lovely thick, dark onion gravy. As I expected, he had brought enough food to survive a siege of four months: boxes and tins stuffed all over the camper. Our friends looking at our overflowing kitchen always joked that Granville could open a corner shop without having to buy-in any more stock. I guess it is something to do with having lived through the Second World War with its rationing.

We were warm and snug after doing numerous manoeuvres and antics to get the bed organised and the gas heater working. We fell asleep to the sound of the wind, sea and seagulls.

I feel this is going to be a very special holiday and yet still have a detached unreal feeling and a few misgivings. Granville, on the other hand, is so happy: he chatters excitedly until his words give way to snoring!

We wake to a cold misty morning. My first thoughts are of the office.

I hope the weekend ladies have got all the new listings and that someone will help them should they need assistance with viewings. Did I remember to leave an advertising list for them? I will have to phone later and find out.

The calm sea is a pale grey-blue. Far in the distance, we can just make out the higher buildings of Eastbourne. When I first arrived in England with Allan in 1996, it is there that we discovered what I still maintain is the best fish restaurant in England. We take every opportunity to return.

"Two cod and chips with onion rings and mushy peas, please."

When the little waitress sees us coming in the door, she has already written out our order and is heading for the kitchen! After a particularly delicious lunch that first day of our sabbatical, we return to the van to pack away some fruit we had bought. I could smell gas! I have the nose of a bloodhound. It makes up a bit for poor hearing, I guess. Granville thought it could be the gas heater, which seemed faulty when he had tried it the previous evening. I have always been hugely respectful of gas. How many times in England do you hear that some poor soul has been blown out of their bed or had some horrible experience with gas? It is only recently that Granville has persuaded me to accept gas heating and a gas cooker in our home. I am wide-eyed with panic! It has got to be fixed! We had all kinds of stupid conversations and questions like…

"Will we have to abandon ship so early in the day? Is it going to cost us a mint to sort out the problem? Have we been sold a dud motor-home?"

Added to the last query were many damming comments from Granville about secondhand car/camper salesmen all being tarred with the same brush! It was getting dark. We found a campsite further west along the coast, outside Littlehampton (The Tudor Rose Campsite). The plan was to spend one more night in Sussex before driving drive back up to Surrey to return to the company that sold us the van. It was a cold night without heating!

17th March

"Let them sort it out…the bugger probably saw us coming," said Granville grumpily, narrowly missing an old granny about to cross the road in a small town along the way back to the garage early the next morning.

The mechanics at the camper company called their 'gas expert' to attend to the problem. While Granville was talking to them in the workshop, I phoned the Global office. Susan was pleased to hear my voice, and she had several queries for me. She persuaded me to sort out a problem between the buyer and seller of a Victorian cottage. It felt important to be needed and vital to the running of the operation. I saw Granville returning. Interrupting her, I said, "Must go! Granville is on his way back! I will phone the clients later. Just text me if you want any more help."

"Okay," she whispered back.

The gas heater was repaired. Granville was smiling.

"It is just as well I have a wife with an excellent sense of smell, or we may have died in our beds!" said Granville smugly as we set off again.

Now we are happy bunnies—horror predictions and threats all forgotten. We set off down the M3 to Bristol, over the suspension bridge into Wales, making our first stop for lunch overlooking the beautiful Wye Valley. Daffodils were starting to appear, and tiny spring lambs dotted the countryside.

Driving on, we found a campsite further up the valley in fields behind a farmhouse near Hay-on-Wye. We knocked several times on a door marked 'office', but there was no response. As we were about to return to the camper, an upstairs window was flung open and someone shouted,

"Just park anywhere!"

We went back several times to pay for our site, but there was no response. The place seemed to be deserted. Later, after supper, we went to a pub down the road. Only the bartender was around. No-one else came into the pub for the hour we were there. The only voices we could hear were the newborn lambs complaining that 'outside mum' was really much colder than 'inside mum'.

"Is it always so quiet here?" we asked the barman was we were leaving.

"No!" he said sharply.

We waited for an explanation, but none was forthcoming. We tucked an envelope with our camping fee into the post-box outside the office and left without seeing another soul.

Morning! Outside was white and frosty, but our camper (especially with its mended gas heater) had proved really warm and comfortable. After breakfast, I went to the amenities block and met a chatty cleaner. My strange accent is usually a conversation opener in England, here in Wales even more so!

"Where are you from, dear?"

After explaining that I came from South Africa (and also *where* it was—she thought it was near Spain!), she told me that the owner's sister had been murdered in Egypt two days before and that the family were understandably in turmoil. Their pub and campsite business were not a priority at the moment. My heart went out to the family, knowing that each would be changed and become different people from who they'd been before the tragedy.

Next day, we drove on towards the western coast of Wales and, at sundown, found the most amazing camping spot atop the cliffs of Lower Fishguard. What a site! Really well equipped! We'd never expected to find such spotless amenities: washing, ironing and other facilities, including an excellent little shop. Being early in the season, there were very few people staying at the site, just a few retired folk who lived in some of the large static caravans for a few months of each year. The owner is typical of the Welsh that I have come across: reserved and quietly spoken, conversation guarded.

Our site overlooked the bay, looking towards upper Fishguard. As night fell, the moon-lit sea, silver and breathtaking, together with the soft cries of seabirds (rather like their human locals, reserved and gentle), gave me the first sense of peace since leaving home. I was starting to relax; so was Granville. But he was still talking! Mostly still about the Bush/Blair war! And I was still in regular contact with the office.

I must try to stop worrying about the office. It is not my problem for a while. I am on holiday!

19th March

We set off along a winding cliff-top path. Soon we reached a little sign that said 'Lower Fishguard' and another 'Upper Fishguard.' Neither gave distances. The sea, far below the path, was sparkling blue, the craggy cliffs awe-inspiring. Delightful spring lambs leapt about in green fields, baaa-ing a welcome, looking at us with their silly, dumb eyes. One poor thing had a sore leg, and I wanted to hop the fence to help it.

"Leave it alone; its mother will probably butt you off the cliff if you go near it," warned Granville.

For the first hour of our walk, we were totally enthralled. Granville led the way, being much fitter than I. God knows how he can talk, walk and climb all at once! The second hour was trickier:

the magnificent views and darling lambs became less interesting. What started as 'just a short walk to work off a huge bacon and eggs breakfast' was now becoming a serious hike. (Remember, I am not an enthusiastic athlete.) For the last leg of the expedition, the lovely sights were totally ignored while I battled for breath, oblivious to everyone and everything except survival whilst making sure I did not fall over the cliffs to smash to bits on the sharp rocks below.

Finally, we turned a corner and saw below us a quaint fishing village. Lower Fishguard! We joined the road down into the village, and after sitting on a bench for a few minutes to recover, we hunted for a tea-room. There weren't any. The only pub in town was closed, so we set off back up the hill. Nursing our aching legs and blisters, we arrived back at the campsite.

"God knows how I will be able to move tomorrow. I have never walked so far in *all* my life," I gasp, clutching the camper bumper.

20th March
Over breakfast, Granville tells me that it's Farmers' Market Day in Upper Fishguard. Apart from talking, he loves to shop. He can sniff out a market within a radius of a hundred miles. After yesterday's hike, (believe it or not) I can still move, but there is no way I am walking to Lower Fishguard and then on to Upper Fishguard, which is up a precipice.

I am looking forward to investigating the picturesque town so suggest that it will be a good opportunity to experience the Welsh bus service. With that, before he could stop me, I go off to find a bus timetable in the campsite communal lounge only to find, to my horror, that the only bus for that morning was due to arrive at the top of the long drive from the site to the main road within fifteen minutes. We set off up the hill at a furious pace. Granville rushed ahead, constantly telling me that I will have to speed up or we will miss the bus. Time to try out some serious power walking! It nearly killed me, but I made it. I thought my lungs would burst, and my face was burning hot. Then some people from the campsite pulled up and asked us if we wanted a lift! I couldn't speak but nodded to accept their kind offer. Just then the bus sped past.

Upper Fishguard is a pretty, colourful town. There are lots of interesting shops of all kinds, and the weekly event is in full swing. I can see that it's more than a market—friends meeting friends, groups of people with heads together talking and laughing. Granville disappears into the thick of it like a happy fish back into its pond.

He enjoys all the rituals of shopping: chatting to shop or stall keepers and discussing and comparing methods of cooking as well as the attributes of such boring things as cabbages, parsnips and mincemeat. Along with the local housewives, he will squeeze, prod, sniff and taste the produce. He *always* buys tons of stuff, much more than we can eat. Later, I see him labouring under piles of farm produce and purchases of all kinds. Once again his hoarding habits for World War Two have taken over. I don't try to distract a happy man!

I found a gorgeous hand-knitted cardigan of an unusual rusty colour then I ambled off down a cobbled road, enjoying the charming ambience of the old town. I discovered art galleries, craft shops, and then a tea-room and the most delicious cup of tea!

Tea is essential to my survival. What makes such delicious tea? Is it the water, the method of preparation, or the actual tea?

I was pondering these hugely important issues when Granville found me (he knew where to look). While we were eating our buttery Welsh cakes, Granville asked me, "Annie…do you want to go to Ireland? It's just across the water to Rosslare in Southern Ireland. The ferry leaves from the harbour."

"Pleeeeees…" I said with a mouth full, crumbs flying out over the table. For years, I had been longing to see Ireland. Granville's family origins are in Ireland, and my granny Lucy-Jane had Irish roots. Then there is this interesting little book in our library at home. It's written by one of Granville's ancestors—great, great, great uncle Herber Shannon. It tells the sad story of two Shannon brothers who were drowned in 1876 when their yacht, Hermit, floundered on Lough Derg and sank. They were trying to save the life of a local man who had gotten into difficulty during a storm. The boys' father was the rector of the local church, and the book tells that a monument was erected to honour the heroic deed.

"One day we will visit that place," I had told Granville when I first read the strange tale.

"Don't bother—it's probably a lot of hogwash," had been his response.

After tea, we set off down the steep hill in the direction of Fishguard harbour to book our tickets. An old dear galloping past (I promise you she must have been expecting a telegram to honour her 100th birthday from the Queen any day) told us that it was a short way down the hill. After a half-hour of strenuous walking down a precipitous road, we reached the ferry ticket office and booked for the trip to Ireland. I told Granville I was definitely not climbing back up into Upper Fishguard town from the harbour, so we waited for a bus. I think he was relieved to get on the bus too.

21st March

As the sun rose the next morning, we were already walking along the cliffs. The sea was far below us as we skirted its edges. The breathtaking views around every bend were pure soul food, and the fresh sea air was a tonic for our lungs, which, for the past few years, have been sucking in the polluted air of the M25 around London.

Within a few feet of the cliff, a farmer was ploughing, the harrow slowly cutting the soil. Seagulls followed behind the tractor, squabbling to get the juicy worms that the blades churned to the surface.

I can't believe I am actually enjoying this long walk. After only a few days exercise, we are much fitter but certainly not thinner. The intake of local produce (Welsh lamb is amazing) and their baking is impossible to resist and makes losing weight highly unlikely. What the hell…we are on holiday! The freedom from time constraints is such a treat but takes some getting used to. I am battling with the absence of deadlines. I feel like there is something I should be doing. I come round with a start.

Have I forgotten to phone/e-mail/see someone? Am I going to be late for that appointment?

Then with equal shock, I realize that there aren't any. I can do precisely what I want. There are no deadlines. This morning before we left for the walk, I nearly phoned the office to see how things are going. Granville was hanging around, so I didn't make any calls, and now, after the walk, I am so glad. I have to keep reminding myself over and over again: *Relax! Don't even think about the office.*

But it's not easy to undo the years of programming.

By Friday afternoon, we had been on the road for a week. The laundry bag was growing like a fat little bug, so I needed to find out how the campsite laundry functioned. I set off, laden with dirty laundry, washing powder, fabric softener and coins for the washer. Firstly—horrors—I discovered that you have to operate the machine yourself. I had no idea of how it worked. I loaded the machine, put money in the little money-shaped gaps, and pressed every knob or lever that looked like the start button. The machine was silent as I struggled to get it to work. I was getting more and more cross.

Shucks…you need to be a rocket scientist to get this thing working.

An elderly lady with curlers in her hair and a huge basket of washing arrived in the laundry.

"You battling, Ducks?" she asks.

She leaned over the machine and pulled a leaver towards her, rammed the coins into the slot again—this time with considerable force—and the machine growled into action. Turning to me, she declared in a strong Lancashire accent, "There you are, love!"

"Thank you so very much," I said, feeling a total idiot. "I'm not a very practical person!"

She nodded and shuffled out, her bunny slippers flopping. I sat on the grey plastic chair in the laundry.

It is so easy at home. You just pile the dirty washing up on the kitchen floor, open the little round door, bung in the whites, colours and the non-iron (separately and in that order), and the machine does its thing. Everything is just where you want it and drying it—no problem.

Walking back to the camper with the heavy load of washing balanced on my head, it suddenly dawned on me that there was no windy-dry or tumble-drier to toss the wet bunch of clothes into.

"How the hell do I dry this lot?" I shouted out loud at a stripy cat sitting on a rock. She looked up at me with an 'its your problem buddy' look and turned her back. Now, if there is anything I can't stand, it's washing hanging around. At home, it must be on the line, in the tumble drier or in the drying cupboard. Having it festooned around the caravan all day was not going to make me happy. I then realised that our bed linen (pure white cotton embroidered with blue forget-me-not) needed to be steam ironed, and so it was not suitable for camping, nor were my linen shirts and drawstring trousers. Later that week, I bought some easy-care, brightly patterned sheets, pillowcases, duvet covers and non-iron track suits. I put away the fashionable white cotton and linen.

Showering was another challenging experience too. I have

always loved to bathe—to lie in the bubbles and wallow for at least an hour. I think the only times in my life I have taken a shower were after swimming or after shampooing my hair (to get all the conditioner out in a final rinse). The campsite did not have a bath. My first attempt was a startling experience. I arrived at the shower block and undressed in what felt like a fridge. Naked (and freezing cold) I started towards the shower, which was separated from the undressing area by a plastic curtain. The water, too, was ice cold and cut off after twenty seconds. The choreography went something like this:

Press the shower button.

Wet the body.

Soap the body and wash.

Press the shower button to wash and rinse off the soap.

Soap back, legs and feet.

Hit the shower button again!

Bend down to retrieve the soap.

Slap the shower button.

Turn the body upside down to get soap off more secluded parts.

Hold shower button on with elbow while rinsing off water.

At this stage of the operation, my numb body registered that the water was getting warmer.

Bliss!

I stood in the warm water for ages, thawing out. Then, as I reached for my razor to shave my underarms, I decided this would be too much of an exhausting labour. I would wait until I found a campsite with a bath. Dripping but clean, I returned to the dressing area to find that I had left my stuff too close to the shower curtain, and my towel and clothes were sopping wet.

As I walked back to the camper after my first ablutions, the sun was setting over the bay. Below, the sea was soft, smooth, silky and silver. The lights of Lower and Upper Fishguard were beginning to twinkle. I stopped, shivering but enthralled and said, "Thank You so much, God. Thank you for the joy of this beautiful rugged place, the view that I have time to enjoy, the freedom from the urgency of business and clean pure air. Thank You for time to stop and stare. Thank You, God."

I am sure I will get used to the lack of some home comforts.

On Saturday, Granville had some shopping to do, so off we set again, this time early enough to walk to the bus stop. Being a less hurried journey than before, we take in the view over the campsite and bays as we walk up the hillside.

Hey...things are changing. It would have been a major schlep a few weeks ago, and now I am finding that it is no longer huff-and-puff stuff to walk up a hill. This is good.

Granville was talking non-stop. This time he was running through all the meals we had eaten since we took off for our sabbatical, explaining the nutritional merits and why we should in fact be getting much thinner.

"We are having tons of salads, fresh vegetables and fruit. *Nothing* that can fatten you up, Annie!"

I reminded him that one of the largest land animals (the elephant) lives on salads (tree leaves), and the biggest sea creatures live on plankton. Later when I could get in a few more words, I added, trying to get the point across,

"Granville, I think the *volume* of food we eat also counts."

Upper Fishguard is a delightful town to walk around. Even though it was our second visit, there was still so much more to see. The aromas of coffee, baking, cooking, mingled with the scent of sea and harbour, create and recall particular memories. A good sense of well-being! (Much of my childhood was spent at the seaside.)

From just two trips into town, I was already on nodding terms with the locals. The Welsh people were guarded at first, but when they discovered we were not English (our accents were a giveaway) they were much friendlier. I thought England and Wales to be one friendly, united country. Sadly this doesn't appear to be the case. As soon as we told them we were South African they warmed. It did not take long for people to express their resentment of the English and what their politicians were doing to Wales. I keep my head well down: UK politics are not my strong point. And anyhow, I like Blair. I think he's got guts.

The Welsh appear to me to be distinctly different from the English in several ways. There is a reserve and a quiet strength. I felt that newcomers to the area would be considered outsiders for years. Nevertheless, we found that the curiosity regarding our origins was an icebreaker. There are few fair-skinned people or blond heads, but there is a predominance of brunettes—mostly with lovely dark brown eyes. I am sure a genealogist would have an intelligent explanation for their predominant features. For myself, I enjoyed engaging them in conversation, listening to the musical Welsh accents.

I found a small wool shop and remembered that I promised to make Gregory a blanket. I bought wool in various shades of blue from navy to baby blue and a crochet hook.

It's at least thirty years since I last picked up a crochet hook. Hope I can still do this thing!

Later in the day we phoned the boys. Allan is very excitedly hunting out a new bike. His transport at the moment is a motocross bike. Those formidable high seated knobbly-tyre things! I hate them. I wish he would get a car, but even they are only marginally safer in the hands of these speed-mad inexperienced drivers.

Gregory was busy preparing for his trip to South Africa. He was going to take Patty to Cape Town first before spending a few days driving up the beautiful Garden Route: a journey which would take them to Plettenberg Bay, Knysna and Grahamstown. The Cape Province has stunning scenery; the hotels, bed-and-breakfasts and tourist shops are super. I am probably biased, but the standard of service and openhearted desire to please guests or visitors generally excels any in Britain and most areas of Europe that we have visited. Most people returning from holidaying in South Africa comment on this high level of service.

Patrick was having trouble with asthma. When he was little, we often had to get him onto a nebuliser or even, in extreme attacks, rush him to the nearest hospital. We found that, apart from stress, dust and pollens, it was almost certainly food additives (especially tartrazine) and dairy or wheat products that caused his breathing difficulties. I thought he might have outgrown the problem, but recently he said that he was back on the asthma pump and antihistamines.

"Hey Patrick," I asked when I phoned him from Fishguard, "will you do me a huge favour? In our hallway bookshelf downstairs, there is a small book called *The Woe of Lough Derg* written by one of your forefathers, Herber Shannon. Please skim-read it for me and answer the following questions: In what town was the monument to the two drowned brothers? Does the book give a church or graveyard name and its locality? What were the boys' names? What year did it all happen? Where was the rectory or manse where their family lived? Can you let me know in a day or two? We are off to Ireland this week."

"No problem!" he said. "I will try to get all the info for you this evening."

And I know he will. When I want something done, I know I can rely on Patrick to do it.

Today is Sunday; we woke late and started the day with bible reading, which we have done since setting out from home. For the first time since our marriage (nearly thirteen years ago), we are getting to grips with the bible together. I have had the privilege of years of good solid ministry, having been brought up in the Plymouth

Brethren. This is a small Christian group known for their strict adherence to simple early church doctrine and knowledge of the scriptures. Granville is getting really excited by what he is finding in the Good Book. I feel a great need to nourish my soul too. I have neglected my spiritual life with business responsibilities and the day-to-day slog of everyday life.

We take a leisurely walk back along the cliffs to the little private cove we found a few days ago and I get to thinking more about my life.

We do the busy life thing, and we forget the most important. We have hungry souls and hungry families. They both need to be fed with our time and attention or their growth is stunted. One of my deepest regrets, looking back over my life, is that I did not spend enough time communicating with my Father (heavenly) and with my friends and family. My mom and dad, both my grannies and grandpas, and several dear friends are dead. It is too late to spend time with them. More deeply painful than the sadness I have over other losses is the fact that I will never have the opportunity to watch Lucy grow up through the years. There had been some urging in a secret part of me that encouraged me to pay her more attention than I did the other children and make the most of the time I had with her. I have no regrets, but I know too that the most valuable gift you give to your children is your time: not things, not money, but just being around for them.

How hugely important it is to laugh, to dance, to talk, to touch and to play, to allow and encourage your children to believe in themselves. It is vital that they know that no matter what they do, you will always love them even though you may hate the bad things that they do. Tell them to get up when they fall—carry on, keep on and tough it out…don't give up!

I recall my mother's positive philosophy and remember the

many times she spent with us leaving chores undone. The housework could wait. She gave us her time. She taught us how to see the funny side of life, how to enjoy people, how to be strong and stand up for what we believed in and to not let anything get us down. I can still hear her say, "Tough times don't last; they'll soon be past."

"Cowboys don't cry—they just shoot their horses." One expression I can't fully explain, but I know it meant that you must not let life get you down... keep your head high, and always look smart is:

"Never let your braces dangle."

"Smile! Nothing hurts forever." Trust me, she was wrong on that one!

Our careers, social life and other ambitions can distort our thinking. It nearly did with me. Chasing the next promotion: a deal or target can make one forget that whilst you are busy, someone else is shaping your child's thinking; someone else is enjoying watching them develop and grow; more frightening, someone else could be damaging them in one way or another, and someone else may be paying your husband/wife the attention you're not! I also know that my business achievements will be forgotten, but time spent 'growing' my children will never have been wasted. I hope I have not wasted too many irretrievable moments. That comment from my friend Vanessa, soon after I separated from my first husband, gave me a dig in the ribs.

"If you don't give these kids some of your time, instead of living at the office, they are going to turn into brats."

In 1987, with Lucy and Allan in tow, I left my first husband. The kids and I had some mad times learning to do without many of the luxuries we had taken for granted. Our lifestyle changed completely. From the large house in the posh suburb, the horse riding, full time maid and gardener, we moved into a small terrace house with a garden that could hardly keep me occupied for a half an hour a week. Forget the need for a gardener. Allan, who was only nine at the time, became the man of the house: wiring plugs and doing the practical jobs. He nearly electrocuted us several times because his knowledge of wiring was rather primitive.

I look back with gratitude that I got to focus on them and enjoy time with them—more especially because Lucy had so few years. I am so fortunate to have met Granville—I was (and am) sure of him and sure of his love.

ନ୍ଧ

We reached a little cove with a soft sandy beach. I realised that Granville was talking. I had not heard a *word* he was saying, but I feared that he had been talking non-stop from the time we set out.

I hope I haven't missed something important!

We put our knapsacks down. Granville settled down amongst the dry seaweed and rocks and was soon snoring so loud, it echoed above the sound of waves coming in over the sand and rocks. I go and paddle in the water, looking for shells and at the sea life surrounding my pink feet. We are the only ones on the beach, enjoying the peace and the absence of traffic and 'people noise'. We eat our lunch of salads and fruit, watching the tide come in. Hours later, we slowly retraced the path and returned to the campsite.

On Monday, the weather was not brilliant. Granville was chatting to the chap who owns and runs the campsite. He explained that it has been unseasonably warm and sunny, so we have been lucky to have had so many hot days! We spent the day by taking a drive to investigate some costal towns further north. Our first stop is Cardigan. It's a charming town, and I find a large sable watercolour-painting brush. Granville finds a bakery and comes to meet me, trying to hide the little packets that no doubt will contain some goodies that will add more lumps to my bum.

We travel on up to New Quay and have fish and chips. It was the worst I have ever tasted: greasy and slimy. The fish was full of bones, and it cost double the amount we pay in our favourite fish-and-chip restaurant in Eastbourne! The view over the harbour was very pretty, but many of the shops were closed, as if the whole town was waiting for something. It had a deserted, gloomy feeling.

When it comes to visiting unfamiliar places, I always feel an excitement—that just around the corner there may be the most amazing view, place or feature. So whatever my feelings are about a place—or anyone else's for that matter—I always enjoy experiencing new places. As we drive along, it dawns on me that today, for the first time, I haven't been continually worrying or thinking about the office, my boss or my clients.

That evening, Patrick phoned. He has read the little book and has the answers to my questions. I now have far more detail to direct me to the vicinity of the events recorded in *The Woe of Lough Derg.*

"Thanks Patrick—you are such a star."

I am determined to find the place where all this stuff happened. Granville was so disinterested I could have kicked him.

"It is highly unlikely that we will find that monument—it'll be like looking for a needle in a haystack. It's bound to be a local legend or just a sad story, but if you want to spend our holiday scampering after a fable about some of *my* dead ancestors, be my guest...you're welcome!"

All this was said in the 'toff' British accent he assumes when he is trying to dissuade me from doing something by simultaneously making me feel like the village idiot for attempting it. It only succeeds in making me more determined.

25th March

We pack up, stow everything away securely and drive down the steep hill to Fishguard harbour, where we board the ferry to Rosslaire in Southern Ireland. Later, over coffee in the ferry lounge, we sit discussing our visit to Ireland as a group of gifted Irish-American musicians sing and play whimsical folk music in the opposite corner. Granville has not been to Ireland for over forty years. I have never been. Later, we were joined by an Irish chap who asked where we came from. On hearing our response, he launched into a tirade about South Africa.

"I hear that the blacks are like savages, slaughtering the whites. You can get shot as you step off the plane. My friend saw bodies all over the place…it's a bloodbath…the whites should strike back. Don't you think?"

I was too angry to answer. He was, by appearances, a successful business man, but so very ignorant about my home country. Uncharacteristically, I am not sucked into this conversation about South Africa. There is too much to tell, and he will not understand it anyhow.

Finally, we docked in Rosslaire and disembarked, but it was too dark to see much. We had planned to find a lay-by soon after leaving the ferry where we could stop for the night. We soon found that all the lay-byes have height restriction bars across the top of their entrances, so we had no choice but to push on to an official campsite. The first we found was at Carrick-on-Suir. According to our camping-site books, this was the only one for miles and miles around that would be open at this time of the year. We were pretty tired and, after an enormous pasta meal, we bedded down to sleep.

3

Sunsets in Ireland

We are woken by the sound of poultry: roosters crowing, hens clucking, ducks quacking, as well as many other unidentifiable animal noises. The friendly owners (farmers, for sure) told us that the reason why there are barriers across the pull-offs and lay-byes in Ireland is that there are hoards of travellers/gypsies who, given the opportunity, just make themselves at home and pitch there for months at a time. When they leave, there usually remains such a mess in their wake, which not only angers the locals who resent these visitations, but also spoils the beautiful countryside.

We drove through a misty, blurred landscape. The route via Clonmel, Mitchelstown and Mallow looked interesting, but we wanted to make our next overnight stop in a less inhabited area. I am surprised at how different it is from England. I had imagined that it would be similar to the countryside of England and Wales, but the architecture and general style of the towns are more like little villages of France. It's also untidy.

There seems to be a huge amount of upgrade to roads and burgeoning housing development. This is frequently advertised as being funded by the European Union, their blue boards with a circle of stars boasting of their assistance in the projects. Many of the houses being built are large and impressive.

Residential housing is mixed with industrial sites, farm buildings that, in turn, jostle alongside factories, shops and commercial enterprises randomly scattered. I guessed that their town planning structures are less defined than those in England: certainly far more relaxed than in South Africa, where we had enormous difficulty in overturning usage or getting planning approval for cheek- by-jowl 'ribbon' development.

We passed through Killarney. Here there were pony-trap rides and a charming town centre with lots of tourist-targeted shops. We followed signs to 'All Routes' and circumnavigated Killarney twice! I (being the navigator) missed the road to Sneem via Muckross, to where we were headed. Finally, on the correct road, we travelled through the Killarney National Park.

This beautiful place is really worth a visit. The views are stunning and can be compared to England's Lake District. It is part of The Ring of Kerry, a heavily plugged tourist route, which takes in the coastline around this spit of land. Granville had to really concentrate to avoid the large, bullying tour buses. We chose to drive the wrong way around! We didn't actually know that all the tour buses and large vehicles were guided in a clockwise direction. We went anti-clockwise, which caused some interesting encounters.

There is a far-reaching view from 'Ladies View'. It's an amazing panorama with the river winding its way hundreds of feet below through a wild and rugged place. It was all such a contrast to the soft green hills we enjoyed earlier.

We were heading for a site that we saw advertised in the AA camping book. The photo looked wonderful – remote and rugged.

"I hope it is as nice in reality as it appears in the book," I commented. "Sometimes these places are photogenic, but in reality, they can be very disappointing."

"It's got to be better than parking in a farmyard," Granville replied, referring to our previous night's stop.

We negotiated narrow roads through stunning scenery, wild hills, lakes, valleys with tough looking sheep grazing on the tufted grasses. The colours were golden autumn tones and the rust-coloured bracken was changing as tiny new sproutings made their springtime debut.

When we arrived at the campsite, we were not disappointed. The setting was stunning. Each stand, set in natural rocky enclaves, overlooked the sea and had its own delightful view. We choose a site within metres from the edge of the water. The tall redheaded owner-farmer came into our van to collect our campsite fees. He explained that his family had lived in the area for generations.

"It's a beautiful place," he said. "Have a look at the historic sites around here as well as the scenery. Just down the road is the home of Daniel O'Connell."

"The Irish ballad singer?" I asked.

"No, no, no…" he said, his Irish accent rolling, "I mean Daniel O'Connell, the man who liberated Ireland from the tyranny of the English at the turn of the century."

I hastily said that I wasn't English. I was from South Africa. The look of thunder and exasperation quickly faded from his ruddy features.

"Oh…that'll be all right then!" he said, and left us to the sound of the lapping waves and sea-bird cries.

We woke up next morning to glorious weather and a stunning view! Last evening's clouds had lifted to reveal soft mauve-blue mountains across the glassy blue water, bays edged with houses painted in a variety of bright hues and clinging to the hillside, craggy coves and sandy beaches, and an amazing panorama of colours and textures in this special place. I felt, as I breathed it all in, that I was at a banquet of beauty. We walked for about half an hour along the coast road to Catherdaniel village. Granville found the local grocery shop tucked away in a pub, and then we continued on down the road to find the home of Daniel O'Connell, the Liberator of Ireland. For an hour, we followed a sign outside the shops in the village that read: *Home of Daniel O'Connell – 1 Mile*.

They must measure miles differently in Ireland!

We turned back and limped home without finding Daniel's home. It was an extraordinarily hot day.

The ablutions at *this* campsite were clean and modern—very well appointed. Unfortunately, I discovered (when I was stark naked) that the showers needed money to operate them, and I had to get dressed, return to the camper and find some coins. Even more irritating, neither of us had any change, so I had a very interesting wash in the hand-basin, requiring contortions that would have been envied by yoga devotees.

At least the water was piping hot!

28th March

As I write, we are still 'moored' at Catherdaniel. We woke this morning to annoying drizzly rain. Granville wanted to get some groceries (God knows what he buys all the time) and post some cards. We drove into Sneem, a picturesque little place. Granville happily disappears into a bakery, and when I turn a corner, I see him diving into another grocery store. Meanwhile, I find a delightful old shop selling local handicrafts, wonderful linen, hand knitted jerseys, paintings, fudge, butter biscuits and delicious Irish chocolate.

Yum!

Granville finds me just as I am paying for a pile of stuff.

"Just a few odds and ends for the kids and Kate," I confess sheepishly. "And chocolates and biscuits for us," I add quietly.

In the afternoon, the rain was heavier, but we returned to Catherdaniel in the camper, determined to find the home of 'The Liberator'. We finally found it—at the end of a long dirt road at least *three* miles from the village where the sign post declares: *Home of Daniel O'Connell – 1 Mile*!

It was not opened to the public, so I walked around the outside of the austere 17th century building—a big rambling home constructed of a mixture of styles which I suspect was evidence of alterations and additions to suit the occupiers of the house over the years. It was rather difficult to describe, imposing and impressive in a quiet, obstinate way. The house was situated 100 yards from a sandy beach and large swirling bay. I walked to the beach, following a grassy path that gave way to sandy dunes sparsely topped with grasses. I sat and gazed out over the wild stretch. It was a breathtaking sight—the beach, lagoon and sea beyond.

There were craggy rocks and boggy inlets with a narrow river running into the sea on the far side of the valley. I noticed signs painted in white on the rocks: *No swimming from these rocks* and *Danger Strong Currents.*

The water looked dark and deep, not a playful place. I could just imagine the Liberator—his face set to the wind, the sea and the future, determining change for his country, planning as he stared out over the wild sea and hills of how to overthrow the impostors and thinking whatever thoughts liberators think.

Somehow in that remote part of Ireland, his tough spirit lurks…it was strong, powerful, inspirational and lonely.

When I returned to the van, which was parked in the parking area for visitors to the house, Granville had prepared a super lunch of tomato soup and whole-wheat bread. After lunch, I begged him to come back with me to the beach and house.

History and ancestors are not his strongpoint.

Reluctantly, he joined me on my second trip to the beach and was seriously impressed. He agreed that it had an extraordinary atmosphere.

"This is awesome," he said quietly.

The following day dawned bright and sunny with not a cloud in the sky. I wanted to try to describe the beautiful tones of the distant mountains and the myriad of colours in the sea. So out came the watercolours for the first time since the early '70s. (For my recent birthday Granville had bought me a painting kit, complete with paper and brushes). Later, my body stiffened into a strange shape, and I found that I had been sitting on the rock lost in my artistic endeavours for two hours. I'd done several paintings on a small sketchpad and thought they were awful. It was frustrating.

It's really difficult to capture the ethereal ambience and tones of the view in front of me. I guess I need a whole lot more practice!

Granville thought my primitive attempts were great!

30th March

Granville and I have been married for thirteen years. It is also Mothering Sunday. I feel very emotional today thinking of my Mum and Lucy. We are in the most beautiful part of Ireland—the part that hugs the coastline. It is a joy to wake up to each morning. After breakfast, we walk along the road again to visit a sandy bay that we'd seen as we drove past on Friday. This campsite is right on the coast, and as I type my diary, I am looking out over the sea to the misty mountains beyond a gentle sea. The colours change hourly, and again I have tried several times to paint the moody view. It's one of the most wonderful places I have ever been. It is so quiet too. I am so happy to be here. But today has some shadows.

I miss my beautiful Lucy and my precious mum: their wild red hair, vibrant personalities, delightful humour and very Irish looks. It hurts to know that they will never see this place. Sometimes the pain of missing them is almost physical.

Allan phoned to wish me happy Mother's Day. He told me that he had forgotten that it was Mother's Day, but they had mentioned it at church. I asked after his brothers and for any other news. He tells me that Patrick and Maxine have found a super flat to rent and that Gregory and Patty have been entertaining friends.

"Don't worry mum, they're all okay." He gave me more family and local news. I got a sweet text from Patrick for Mother's Day. He is so thoughtful: often he seems to sense that I am hurting and will reach out in his special way.

For our anniversary dinner, we go to a pub in nearby called *The Blind Piper*. It was crowded with young and old and had great atmosphere. Someone was playing a musical instrument of some kind; I didn't see what it was, but it was lovely...perhaps it was a fiddle. We had a super dinner with huge servings. I chose seafood chowder and the most delicious melt-in-the-mouth chocolate dessert. Granville started with tomato soup, then lamb and vegetables, which he said was marvellous. Next to our table was a family of five young children with their mom and dad. They were so well behaved. What a pleasure!

We left our lovely mooring early the next morning, continuing around the Ring of Kerry, enjoying spectacular views across the silver bays far below us: Derrynane, Hog's Head and Waterville. We delighted at the unspoilt beaches, little harbour towns, and the sharp dark cliffs. We were grateful that parts of the world had maintained their quiet loveliness despite the cancer of overpopulation. Just before noon, the tour busses arrived; they tore around the narrow roads at terrifying speeds. Frequently, we had to pull aside to let the growling bullies pass. A crusty local we spoke to in a small town told us that the best way to tackle them was to stand up to them and not to move over. He advised: "Stare straight ahead! They don't want to be delayed by an accident; they just want to get around the route as soon as possible to pick up the next batch."

"Easier said than done with tons of 'flash' tourist bus heading right for you!" observed Granville later when we were close to being driven down a steep bank as he swerved to avoid a monstrous coach.

We reached our destination: a small town called Doolin on the far west coast. It is famous for its folk music and wild weather. We found a campsite at Doolin Point, overlooking the quay from where the ferries (now safely moored) cross to the Aran Islands. The campsite was not officially open, but the owner kindly made the grounds and its facilities available to us. We settled the camper and ourselves in then walked back into the village of charming cottages painted bright pink, yellow, green and blue in many tones. Some of the homes and shops were made of local stone, as was the bridge over the river in the centre of the town.

I met a young South African lad from Pretoria working in one of the craft shops. My Afrikaans is not perfect, but soon we were talking away in the unique South African language derived from Dutch. He said that he had met only four South Africans since coming to Doolin! He is a writer, but I sense there is a whole lot more to his story. I enjoy hearing about people's lives.

Why are they so far from home? Are they married, divorced, single? Are they happy, sad, rich or poor? What has happened to them to make them happy, sad, rich or poor? So many intriguing lives! If I am watching someone or, more especially, a couple, their body language speaks louder than anything they may say. It is also really fascinating to watch groups of business people. It is easy to see who is in control, who's the boss, and who wishes they were. I often wonder if a person trying to ingratiate himself or herself with the boss knows just how transparent he/she is to the observer. People reveal so much of their true intentions and feelings by their body language and their mannerisms.

Anyhow, back to this Afrikaans chap; he looks as if he is running. Many South Africans are here to escape the violence or financial squeeze of the new South Africa, where there is still a great deal of civil disobedience and disregard for the law. In the business arena, there is a clear practice of 'affirmative action'. Although I fought vehemently to get rid of the disgusting Apartheid regime, I feel that 'affirmative action' is just reverse racism. It's understandable after all that happened, but nevertheless, it is still a policy that favours certain ethnic groups.

On our walk back to the campsite, the view over the sea is beautiful, but to the south, there is an angry black sky. I think it is blowing this way. We have had mostly glorious weather since we left home. Both in Wales and here in Ireland, people have commented that the weather has been unseasonably great for this time of the year. Apparently, it is unusually early in the spring to have sunny days without much rain.

At supper that evening, the wind was howling. The van was being buffeted around, and it was pelting down fat noisy rain drops. Granville went out to move the camper to face into the wind. The rocking and rolling lessened, but it rained right up until after lunch the next day. We really didn't mind. It was good to catch up with writing and reading.

Amazing—it's three days since I heard from any of the Global offices.

1st April
It was a wild, stormy day, but the amazing views more than made up for the weather! The campsite was ideally situated for far reaching views of the bay, and to our left were the cliffs of Moher. We were protected from behind by emerald green hills. After breakfast, once again we walked into Doolin. The turbulent sea was a strange green-blue in places and dark Prussian blue in others, but as it thumped against the cliffs, it churned up to a creamy white spray and foam. The farms along the way seemed to blend country and coast. Fat cows huddled against grey stone walls, ignoring the beauty as they slowly,

thoughtfully chew the cud. We saw a big brown hare. She noticed us and scurried up and over the stone wall. I hadn't seen one so close up before. She had a comical intelligent face. It was delightful to watch her.

The next day, the weather was still inclement, so we decided to take a drive along the coast towards Galway. Our tour takes us through Lisdoonvarna, a small spar-town that has a romantic matchmaking festival each September. This tradition was started long ago by the rich farmers and landowners who wanted to marry off their children. Hundreds still congregate for these fun-filled days, and a king and queen is chosen.

Heading towards the coast, we found the landscape changing dramatically into a rocky, surreal world. This area is called The Burren, and it is one of Ireland's most unique areas—also one of the few examples of Karst limestone in Europe. It almost resembles a lunarscape in its most isolated areas and presents a stark contrast to the mountains or lush green hills most associated with Ireland. This area is of particular interest to botanists and geologists as well as to the general public—a fascinating place.

We drop down to a sweet little town called Ballyvaghan before going on to Kinvara, a delightful little fishing town. The bright colourful cottages and lovely small harbour have a quaint design when seen along with the architect-designed modern buildings. A gentle blend of new and old. I bought a pottery vase and hand-made shawl for Kate (my sister). The shop owners all along the way in Ireland could be the subject of a book on their own: so varied, incredibly interesting and from many walks of life. They were always welcoming—especially when they heard we were from South Africa.

We should have spent more time in and around the little villages and enjoyed the peaceful coastline because when we reached Galway, the traffic was horrible. Granville had a 'frothy'! He was so irritated by the traffic that we drove straight out of town, stopping for lunch overlooking what was supposed to be 'Galway Bay', but which, in reality, was an expanse of smelly mud-flats. The song my mother enjoyed (by someone called Ruby Murray) which tells of the beautiful Galway Bay must refer to another Galway Bay! Or maybe we were seeing it from the wrong angle.

4th April

The weather was foul. Wind was still smashing huge waves against the cliffs—magnificent to view from the safety and warmth of the camper, but not the kind of weather to tour around or to spend time outdoors, so we wrote, read, crocheted (Gregory's blanket), ate and drank copious amounts of tea and coffee.

It may be the right time to describe our travelling home. Granville did a marvellous job of fitting it out. It's not new—probably about 10 years old. The overall length is just over twenty-two feet. It has a loo (chemical flushing action) and a shower in one cubical, also a small hand basin. There is a water heater provided; so as long as we remember to pre-heat (gas or electric), we get really hot water. There is a hanging cupboard, a cooking and wash-up area (stove, oven, grill and sink, and drawers for utensils), storage above and around the 'walls' and storage below the seats at the far end of the cab. These seats create the most magic large (6'6" x 6') bed for the night time. All very cosy! Granville has added extra fixtures and fittings to enhance our day-to-day living. These include lights over the bed, a wonderful sound system throughout the van, extra storage, machinery and technology, and, last but not least, a T.V. (for Granville)!

Late in the afternoon, we walked into the village of Doolin. The wind pulled at our clothes and whipped our carrier bags to fly behind us like kites. We first called at the grocers and then visited the folk music shop, where we spent some time both looking at books of the history of Irish music and listening to recordings of this unique harmony. It was our last evening before leaving the area; we sat in a charming little pub, enchanted as a pipe and fiddle players displayed their repertory of haunting melody, and a singer sang heart-tugging, sorrowful songs.

Allan phoned just after we arrived back in the camper to see how we were. He told me that he was going to get baptised (the full-immersion water baptism) at Holy Trinity, Brompton in London. Nikki Gumble, the prime activator of the (now internationally known) Alpha course had asked Allan to be prepared to give his testimony at the baptism. His conversion is a relief and joy to me.

It was with reluctance that we left Doolin that morning, but I was excited by my quest to follow up on the facts and the places mentioned the little book written by Granville's forefather. From the information Patrick gave me, the church and graveyard are on the banks of the Lough in the town of Mount Shannon. (Our family must have strong connections to the town from its founding days!) The vicar was Augustus Shannon (the drowned boys' father). Patrick gives me the names of the boys and ages: twenty-four and twenty-seven (by strange coincidence, exactly the ages Gregory and Patrick will be in September this year). It is almost a hundred years to the day from when these lads were drowned to when Gregory was born.

We drove firstly through Ennis—a busy town. After parking the camper, we each went our separate ways: Granville to the butcher, bakery, news agency and any other shops he can find whilst I found the most cluttered antique shop, which occupied me for over an hour. After a really great coffee, we continued north via stunning scenery. Here, unlike the wind-torn coast, the countryside was gentle and soft, with old stone cottages tucked along the roadside. We dipped down to the Lough, and following the banks, we arrived in the small village of Mount Shannon, where we asked for directions to the protestant church. We were directed to the parish Church. A notice board just within the walls of the church read: *Church of Ireland: Mount Shannon (Anglican).*

At first, we had difficulty in opening the iron gates into the churchyard. A neighbour who lived next door to the church heard the commotion and told us that the gate just needed brute force. Once applied, it moaned open. As I began my search amongst the gravestones for some connection to the Shannon family, I heard Granville complaining. "Who in their right mind wants to spend all their holiday digging around in a cemetery? This is nothing but a wild goose chase! You don't seriously think this is fun. I must be mad to agree to ferreting around a graveyard in some Godforsaken part of Ireland. The only thing that connects us to this place is our name…"

He stopped mid-stream in his burble when he heard squeals of delight from me. I had found the monument and graves! They were rather overgrown with ivy and shrubs, and the surrounding fencing lay in disarray, but the actual monument stone was tall and impressive. Unfortunately, it is covered with lichen that had damaged the stone. Despite this, the worn old words told the poignant story:

Here lie the bodies of
Charles Henry Shannon
Aged 27 years
And his much loved brother
Augustus Irwin Shannon
Aged 25 years,
Who were the only surviving children of
the Rev. Augstus C L Shannon,
Rector of this Parish.
Who were drowned in Lough Derg
on the 4th September 1876.
Their yacht Hermit having foundered in a
squall between Mount Shannon

and Castle Lough.

'They were lovely and pleasant in their lives and in their death they were not divided'
2nd Samuel Chapter 1 v 23
'And they shall be mine saith the Lord of Hosts in that day when I make up my jewels.'
Malachi 3 v 17

On the reverse side, there were more bible verses and an explanation of how the boys died. The little book filled in some of the gaps, giving the name and further details of the chap who they were attempting to rescue and also told of a premonition that Charles had. He dreamed a disturbing, detailed dream in which he and his brother tried to help another boatman, George Fletcher, and in doing this deed of mercy, their own yacht sank. It was caught in a freak wind with foamy waves. In his vision, he also saw his father walking along the beach—a forlorn and sad figure.

I found it so moving, and Granville had tears in his eyes as he knelt down in the green grass in front of the stones and began to wipe off the moss. He took dozens of photos of the gravestones, monument and church.

Later, the lady who lived in what we discovered was the old school house offered us tea. She had lived in the village all her life, and she said that the story of the heroic boys was well known and that they were reputed to have attended school in that very room. It was also marvellous to imagine the scene many years before. I could almost hear the shouts of the teacher reaching into the carved rafters.

"Wake up…stop dreaming of your boats…concentrate on your sums. Augustus…you will not get to cricket practice until you have finished that chapter. Come on boys…sharp now!"

The quiet broken only by the scratching of the nibs on paper and the teacher walking up and down on the wide plank floors…

That schoolroom was alive with the ambiance of the past.

After tea in pretty bone-china mismatched cups and saucers, we continued down to the banks of the Lough that lay about quarter of a mile from the church. We were both quiet as we ate our soup-lunch, looking over the water. Not written on the inscription but told in the story-book was the heartbreak of the mother and father. We especially found deep empathy for that mother. Wow, it is pain enough to lose one child, but to lose two (or more) must be just unbearable. I wonder if the phrase on the gravestone 'surviving children' was indicative of her having lost *other* babies or children. How did she feel, looking over that water, scanning the Lough towards Holy Island where she last saw the little yacht on its outward journey? Somehow, I feel she knew. It's a heavy feeling—a dry-mouth sick feeling—a sixth sense that prepares you for the awfulness of your deepest pain. How did she cope when the bodies were found and her sons confirmed dead? In this gentle place, I can imagine that hurting mummy with empty arms standing quietly on the hillside, overlooking the little harbour, nursing an ache that time does not heal. She must have been brave and strong of faith for the author of the book to have had such admiration for her.

A mile out of town, we see a sign leading to a Lakeside campsite. Turning down the bumpy, muddy road, we meet the owners— kindly old people who also agreed to open up the campsite for us even though it was officially closed until Easter. Our site was right on the banks of Lough Derg, and we quickly settled in. The finding of Granville's ancestors' home and final resting place of the two young lads occupied our thoughts and minds long into the night.

6th April
It is Sunday, and today seems an anti-climax after yesterday.
Granville is still reliving yesterday's discoveries. It's so good to

see him happy with links to his past, also that he is so thrilled to be on this trip. I don't think he ever expected to touch places in his ancestry that he did not know existed. I too have bonds of empathy with these families and their journeys of yesteryear. I know we are privileged and thank God for this opportunity to look back at the past and enjoy the now.

Our pitch is within a few feet of the Lough, with a view looking out toward Mount Shannon village, its harbour, and out over the water towards Holy Island with its tall stone tower. Later that morning, local families came to enjoy the day on the Lough shore. It is soul food to relax and watch the activities around us: people swimming and boats splashing, swans and other water birds milling around and yachts sailing by on quiet water. After lunch, we walked into town, hoping to find the church open so that we can check church records for more family history. Sadly, the service was over and the church locked, so we walked around Mount Shannon instead. In itself, it's a delightful little town. We feel connected to this place in spirit and in name.

The sunset over the lake that evening was calming, beautiful, and almost spiritually dimensional, the atmosphere of peace and serenity all-encompassing. I cuddle down in bed with gratitude to God for this wonderful holiday, the opportunity to enjoy many new places, and the time to really absorb and recall. I was also expunging sad memories and being refreshed by new experiences.

I can't remember a time in my life when I felt so happy—except when my babies were born.

7th April

Our penultimate day in Ireland.

Granville woke me earlier than usual and said he had a surprise for me. He had hired a boat to row across to Holy Island! From our campsite at the waterside, we could see the misty island across the water. The man who has hired us the boat told us to use the tall tower as a landmark. I was delighted at the thought of going to investigate the edifice and the many ruins one could see from a distance. Soon after setting off, Granville reported that currents and winds seem to be stronger than he had expected. To keep us on target took a great deal of course adjustment and brute strength, with me looking over Granville's shoulder, directing him towards the tower on the near side of the island. The navigation consisted of me instructing, "Stronger to the left…no…bit more to the right…keep on…that's it."

Granville said there was a strange kind of tugging undertow that seemed to be constantly taking us off course, and I could also feel the sharp cross-winds.

"Just as well you aren't a weakling," I said with sincere gratitude.

The trip took almost an hour. We landed near a small jetty. A sign, *Beware of the Bull*, nailed to a tree, greeted us. What an intriguing place! I guess the island was about fifty acres in all, and that time was unpopulated except for a herd of cows (don't ask me who milked them) and obviously a bull (thank God we never met him). Noting many walls and solid remains of ancient inhabitants, we soon come upon three church ruins (one almost intact except for the roof), parts of a small abbey and the tall round tower that could be seen from many miles away. It was a weird chimney-style tower that seemed to serve no purpose except as a marker. We wondered if there were underground tunnels up and into it and stairs winding up to the top: a kind of watchtower, perhaps. There were several brass plaques scattered amongst the ruins that explained that the island has seen inhabitants come and go, in war and peace, for the last 2000 years. There were Bronze Age remnants and evidence that it was a holy retreat for Christian missionaries from the first century. Apparently, Viking invaders occupied the island at some stage of its history too.

We stumbled on (Granville did, literally) a mound: remains of large structures and a well still filled with 'holy water'. We found graves of many generations, including some more recent gravestones alongside the ancient.

This place was also a silent witness to when the Shannon boys drowned. The story in our little book tells that they disappeared just near Holy Island—on the tower side. We ate our picnic in the middle of a green meadow, looking down a peaceful hillside amongst the whispers of the past. As it was getting dark, we felt it was time to leave the island to return to the campsite. I watched as Holy Island became a smudge in the distance behind us. By then the mist was swirling in. I made dinner that evening (mushroom omelette); Granville was totally exhausted and nursing his blistered hands!

We were booked on the ferry to return to Fishguard late the following afternoon but both wished that we could have much more time in Ireland. The soft accents, green grass and contrasting wild rocky coasts, the special open friendly reception that we found everywhere won our hearts. Especially fascinating was the feeling of being connected and belonging. We made an early start from the Lakeside campsite, the camper groaning and grumbling as it took us on the twisty roads around the beautiful Lough. There were lovely towns that we would have loved to have investigated (Killaloe looked especially attractive), but we needed to get across to the east coast to catch the ferry by late afternoon. We made a few stops along the way. Waterford (where the Waterford crystal comes from) and another funny little town called New Ross need revisiting some time in the future.

New Ross has a river harbour, and moored near the town is a replica of the Dunbrody famine ship that sailed from Ireland to America during the potato famine 150 years ago. Many well known and successful American families, such as the Kennedys, trace their roots back to the desperate folk who left for America to seek a better life and a full tummy! One of the passengers listed on the Dunbrody was Patrick Kennedy, the great-grandfather of the late president John Fitzgerald Kennedy.

We boarded the ferry for our return to Wales with a feeling of accomplishment. As we discuss this (it is not our *own* achievements that have brought us satisfaction but rather the awareness we had of the resilience of other people who lived long ago), we realized that these individuals motivate us to be stronger and better and teach us that no matter what happens in life, there is *always* hope.

There is tremendous inspiration in realising that whatever changes or misfortunes there are in our lives, we would always have an opportunity to find fulfilment and a better future provided we were strong and brave and prepared to step out of the comfort zone of familiar territory.

When I thought of the office now, it was with the realisation that change was inevitable; I shouldn't allow my career to completely consume me.

9th April

Just before 3 a.m.! We landed at Fishguard and drove a few hundred yards from where we disembarked. We parked the camper on the quayside to sleep a few hours, hoping that we would not be moved on! Granville was really too tired to travel further.

At 8.10 a.m., I received a mobile phone text from my sister Kate reminding me that it was our Mom's birthday anniversary today. I didn't need the reminder. I had thought about Mom as soon as I woke a half hour earlier. Our lovely mom died in 1998. She was a gutsy lady, a wonderful mum who died with such dignity. I still feel cheated now when I think about her death. I didn't have the opportunity to say goodbye and to tell her how much I loved her. She told *no one* that she was terminally ill with cancer. She warned the doctors that they were *not* to tell her family, and we only heard that she was ill two days before she died. The first inkling that I had of any problem was when my sister Kate phoned from South Africa to say, "Anne! Mom is really, really ill."

Knowing that Kate is the opposite of a drama-queen, I flew over on the first available flight. Mom died before I left England, as I was waiting to board the plane. I only discovered that she was dead when I arrived in South Africa the next day. On the Friday before she died (the day my sister phoned me to say that she was ill) Mom had been admitted to the local hospital some fifty miles from their farm. My brave mom refused all treatment, but she collapsed in great pain, and for the first time in her life, she was admitted to hospital. (My sister and I, in the tradition of the times, were born at home). The next day, she allowed the doctor to tell her family that she was incurably ill. She was suffering with cancer that had invaded her spine, lungs and the bones in her legs, but right up until the last moment, she was still telling everyone, "Don't worry, stop fussing—I'm fine."

Mom loved God and lived a simple life of honesty and directness with Jewish chutzpah allied with tons of courage. She was fun and joyful, and her wicked sense of humour was well known. We enjoyed her from our earliest memories to the last conversation we each had with her. She gave us the basics for strength of mind and coping techniques to face life head on: she gave us backbone. In Fishguard, Wales, five years later, I saluted her, along with my sister Kate in Pietermaritzburg, South Africa. The beautiful orange and pink sunrise that morning over the still harbour was such a fitting tribute to a feisty redhead. One of the two missing from my life and taken away far too early.

Thank You, thank You, God! Thank You for Mom and my beautiful Lucy. Thank you for the time we had with these lovely ones. They were both extraordinary. They were both funny and fun. We feel the depth of loss that can only come from having loved someone intensely.

I sat for a long while looking out to sea.

It was our intention to go back to the campsite in Fishguard for another week, but as we ate our breakfast I said, "Lets go home!"

Somehow, I just needed to go home. Five hours later, we were back in our little terrace house and got to grips with washing, cleaning and getting the van cleared out. There was a mountain of post to sort through—mostly junk mail. And…best of all…I had a long wallow in the bath, soaking until the water was cold enough to top up with more hot water and my fingers and toes went wrinkly.

Joy!

Personal bathing and hair grooming, washing, drying and ironing clothes at home is simple. We won't go in to the delights of the dishwasher. Although camper life was much more fun than I thought it would be, it is not as comfortable as home.

But then…it's much more exciting.

My last thoughts as I fell asleep that first night back:

I hope I don't crawl out of bed in the night and pee in the wardrobe, mistaking it for the loo-cubical in the campervan!

4

Touching Base

To summarize our first three weeks away: They were interesting, hugely enjoyable and increasingly relaxing. The camper-van life would *not* be my first choice of holiday, but I have come to appreciate that it is a privilege and a great joy to travel, and this is probably the most affordable means of transport for us. I am acutely aware that this is such a liberating experience that I shall wish we could spend the rest of our days living with this *kind* of freedom but, may I hastily add, not necessarily in a camper!

Granville is in his element; he just loves every moment of the mobile home experience. I can tell he feels in control of his life, and even at this early stage in the project, he is happier than he has been for many years. As I mooch around the house, I try to analyse what it is that I don't or do like about the camper experience. On the 'don't like' side is: washing myself and clothes, washing the dishes, pots and pans in such a confined area (especially after Granville's gourmet meals), the food smells trapped in the living areas and the small space generally. On the 'like' side: freedom from worry about work, seeing wonderful places, fresh air, walking, relaxing, thinking and praying, reading the Bible, discovering my husband maybe for the first time since we married and time to have fun and laugh. I feel that this is going to be a really worthwhile period of our lives.

Originally, I thought that I would 'put up' with the camper and the outdoor life, and that the only advantages would be that we would be fitter and slimmer. Well, so far we are definitely fitter, but unfortunately, the delicious Welsh cakes, Irish potato cakes and thick clotted cream have negated all the exercise.

For the first three weeks of our trip, I thought about the office often, but the initial cold turkey has passed. I still have regular telephone contact with Global Real Estates and have been woken several times suddenly at some mad hour of the night or early morning

Oh dear Lord...it's the 25th...I haven't prepared the monthly figures!

One afternoon, when we were driving through a remote town in Wales, I froze and panicked.

"Granville...stop! I haven't done the copy for the newspaper advertising. It's Friday, and I've missed the 10 a.m. deadline. Better get hold of the print department now!"

"Calm down, woman! You're on holiday now. Remember?" He smiled but looked at me with a worried expression.

Most of my working life had been so intertwined with the office, with work. But I was slowly mellowing and thinking about it, worrying about it less and less. I wished I could rid myself of the burden that I am personally responsible for the office performance and the frustration that the clients are not being looked after properly when I am not there, which I know is a kind of arrogance.

Later that evening, after arriving back home, I phoned a few friends to catch up on local news. I spoke to Peter (young chap who is fostering kitty) to see how she was doing. Apparently, she was fine; Peter had got her into a more acceptable routine. She mostly woke up for her morning feed at 6.45 a.m., which was about the time that the milk-man called. I still miss her furry wake-up calls, but I was happy that she settled.

The following day, I called into the Ascot office.

"How are things going?" I ask Susan as I sat down at my desk. She was frantically busy preparing a tour-list.

"Can't talk now, Annie, we'll catch up later," she said sweetly.

I sat at my desk, shuffling through the pile of mail that was addressed to me. Within ten minutes, I was ready to run away. The phone was ringing non-stop, a client was screamed down the phone at me because she hadn't received her deposit rebate, the office was hopelessly understaffed, and the poor girls were frantically busy. When I looked for some brochures to send to an inquiry, the sales detail cabinet had not been updated and was out of price order. I checked up on a sale in progress; the vendor was hopping mad because someone had offended the applicant, and he had withdrawn from the sale in high dudgeon. As I put the phone down from hearing of the failed sale, I turned to Susan, amazed that she was so composed in the midst of all the mayhem.

"Sorry, it was a mistake to come in."

"Hummmm…" she said, "and today is one of the quietest for ages. You should have been here last week. It was busy."

"How on earth did I put up with all that crap?" I asked myself aloud in the car on the way back home.

Our little garden needed tidying but still looked pretty with petunias and pansies in full bloom. The clematis and jasmine climbers had just started to trail over the arbour seat, trellises and wooden fence that Granville erected last autumn.

I really love gardens and gardening, but for the past six years have had little time to enjoy it. I have done most of the planning, and Granville is the planter and action man! He is really conscientious and dedicated.

Within the first week of moving into this terrace house, we had dug up and removed most of the previous owner's efforts. It had a modern, minimalist feel: raked chip stone, a terra cotta statue of fat chap (Buddha?), spiky palms, pampas grass and a wooden deck. Left with a naked patch of earth, we started again. We laid a lawn, created flowerbeds, and when Granville's back packed in and he was restricted to hobbling around and issuing orders, Patrick (youngest son) built a super patio of replica York-stones where there had been a slippery deck.

A few weeks later, we planted shrubs, climbers, flowers and trees and added the garden furniture. Now it is looking more like the English country garden I have always wanted. My dream garden is larger...perhaps an acre of land...surrounded by a mossy weathered old wall and encompassing a quintessentially English cottage with hollyhocks against the walls and roses or wisteria around the windows.

The next few days back home pass by quickly. I meet friends for lunches and coffee; the boys visit. Friends and family are curious and especially surprised that I have not abandoned ship. When Granville was not around, I was asked by both the boys and friends from the office, "Are you doing this just for Granville?" "Are you *really* enjoying it?"

I answer honestly. "Well...I miss my bath and my cat, but it's great to get away and have time to appreciate, to pray and to think. I feel that I am getting my mind and soul back!"

13th April
We dropped Gregory at Heathrow for his return to South Africa. We had booked our trip to South Africa for the 12th May, so the parting was not really painful. We would see him in a month.

On Sunday, as I fiddled around in the garden, I noticed that Granville was restless. He was pacing around like a mother cat about to give birth: looking in cupboards, scraping little bundles of stuff together and not sitting in one place for more than a few minutes. He was talking incessantly about how wonderful it was 'on the road' and how much he enjoyed to smell the fresh sea air at the seaside and in the country.

"I can't stand this petrol-laden air," he said, striding out the door to do some shopping, "I am sure it's poisoning my lungs."

"No doubt it is!" I answered.

I think he knew how much I valued my home comforts, and he was poop scared I would abandon the project. When he returned an hour or so later I asked, "Do you want to hit the road, Love?"

I get an embarrassed but grateful look from him. We pack up the wagon, close up the house and get ready for trip two.

14th April

We took off again with a considerably reduced load. Living in the camper had taken some organisation, and for this trip, I had left a lot of clothes and clutter behind. I managed (with considerable effort) to persuade Granville to jettison some cargo.

"Good grief, Granville, don't be so bloody ridiculous! All these boxes of tins of food are totally too much! The emergency equipment you have on board would be the envy of the ambulance service and Red Cross emergency stocks combined. Why carry all this stuff? Wherever we go we will not be too far from a shop."

The final comment seemed to do the trick, and Granville grumpily unloaded several boxes and packets from the storage compartments.

"Well don't blame me if you starve to death."

Highly unlikely!

We found a campsite just outside Eastbourne and booked in for two days. Before we committed ourselves to longer, we decided to try out the facilities…especially the ablution-block. Later, we found that the showers were hot (and free), wash up areas and loos clean and well kitted, and the site was quiet except for the trains that sped by on the far side of the valley. (I am deaf, so it doesn't really bother me.) In fact, I rather enjoy seeing commuters going to and from work.

Poor you! I think dispassionately, sipping tea, still in my stripy pyjamas.

After breakfast the next day, we walked along the promenade of Seaford. We saw the huge cross-channel ferries coming and going on a grey choppy sea decorated with tiny white waves. Later, we did some shopping in Eastbourne before following the road up to Beachy Head, which rises up hundreds of feet above the town. There is a coastal drive (or walk) along a nature reserve following the cliffs. After Beachy Head (also a popular suicide leap), there is Birling Gap with stairs down to the beach far below. It is the most perfect place when the tide is out, and it is awesome when the tide is in as the waves clap against the chalk cliff faces. From there, the road moves away from the coast to East Dene, but you can walk all the way along hills called 'The Seven Sisters' to Seaford.

The sun had come out, and we stopped at the Seven Sisters Country Park, where there is a visitor centre. Parking the camper, we planned to walk from there to the beach about a mile away, following the river. Sheep dotted the landscape, and it was a level, easy walk, but the geography of the area is really remarkable. The river forms a perfect textbook oxbow as it twists and writhes along the valley. At the mouth, there are exaggerated bows and curves. Granville explained (all the way to the beach) the finer points of estuaries, oxbows, tiles, geology as well as geography. Geography was one of his specialist subjects when he was a school teacher. I am sure that what he was saying was very interesting and informative, but I was distracted.

What a beautiful picture! Green hills either side, blue sky above, the river sliding past, herby sheep and sweet bovine

*smells, fresh sea-air perfume, and a symphony of sounds—
bleating, mooing and the sea rasping over pebbles.*

We came across gun batteries and dragons teeth blockades built during the Second World War—evidence that this part of the coast could have provided prime beach landing for invaders. When we reached the pebbly beach, we propped ourselves up against a log and relaxed on the warm stones. It was a gorgeous day…the sea ultramarine blue, gulls reeling overhead like Saturday night drunks. On the way back, I tripped and fell flat on my face (so embarrassing).

What is it about tripping? It is far more humiliating than it should be. When I had picked myself up from the pebbles, blood was running down the inside of my jeans onto my feet, and my palm was cut. I carried on walking, only examining the injuries when I got into the camper. Not too much damage, but it hurt. Tomorrow we must go home to spend Easter with the boys.

Before we return home to Chertsey the next morning, Granville and I part ways. I needed to do some Easter shopping, and Granville wanted to take advantage of the sunshine. Someone told him years ago that he looks like Sean Connery when he has a tan, so he always makes a bee-line for every bit of sunshine he can find. I also need a break from his constant chatter. A friend and I were discussing Granville's loquaciousness, and she said how lucky she thought I was. Her husband (of twenty-nine years) said less and less over the years, and now their communications were reduced to grunts. I suppose I should be grateful that he is mostly cheerful and communicates constantly. The trouble is I often switch off and say 'yes', or more accurately, 'ja' (South African, Afrikaans for 'yes') every ten minutes or so while I am thinking my own thoughts. Sometimes he catches me out! I blame my poor hearing!

I must buy clothes for our trip to SA.

As I tried on trousers and a shirt, I felt disgusted. I couldn't even get into a 20! When I married Granville, I was an 8 (honestly). Over the past thirteen years with all his amazing food (he is a really good cook, and he loves to cook), I am twice the weight I was at forty. I guess menopause and age has added to the problem, whatever the excuse. Having been a skinny for forty years (until I married Granville), I thought it would be fairly easy to get rid of the blubber when I got serious about dieting, but the weight piled on. I got more and more panicky then tried to diet, and the see-saw dieter story became a reality. I can remember in my skinny days when people would talk about losing weight and dieting and how difficult it was, I used to say unsympathetically, "Why can't you just shut your mouth so the food won't go in?"

I am lucky to be alive.

It was good to be home again. I wallowed in a hot, soapy bath and washed my hair. Allan came over to see us, and we walked to Sainsbury's for Granville to 'stock up' and returned as laden as dung beetles. When we arrived back home (my arms were aching from the weight of oranges, apples, coke and so on), Maxine(Patrick's girlfriend) and Patrick were waiting for us, enjoying the sunshine. Later, we had a braai (barbecue), laughed, talked about all the mad family things that have happened, discussed how most South Africans have a completely different outlook to the locals, argued about the war in Iraq and Tony Blair, and generally batted thoughts and opinions back and forth, wanting to share our points of view no matter how rubbish.

We staggered into upright positions when Granville brought out the boulle, and we played the game firstly on our little patch of lawn and then on the chip-gravel around the side of the house. The wonderful sunshine continued all day. The garden looked as pretty as a picture.

We have, each one of us, learned to appreciate family, and it has been good to be together. We have been through some heavy stuff that has given us a deeper appreciation of one another, born out of the knowledge that we are fragile, and time together is to be savoured.

On Easter Sunday, Karin and Peter Flanagan join us for lunch. Peter is a South African doctor whose family origins are Irish, and Karin was born in Ireland but moved to SA when she was in her teens. They have become close and dear friends since we came to England. They've been here for eight years, but we knew them from the local social scene in Hilton, South Africa where we all lived. I must admit, I had initially found Karin rather direct. She may not know it, but she was a reason I broke up with my first boyfriend after I got divorced from husband number one. This is what happened.

I was devastated and heartbroken after the failure of my marriage of fifteen years. Lucy, Allan and I felt like survivors after a horrible storm. My life revolved around my children, my family and work. Within a few months of the messy divorce, I noticed that a local doctor was paying me a whole lot of attention. I was feeling fragile and alone, and he was a willing ear, phoning me morning, noon and night. I soon realized that his attentions were personal; I was attracted to him and we started to date. I must have been a naïve idiot, but the classic attached man dating syndrome followed. Our get-togethers were always during the week (never weekends), we always met at my home, at a restaurant or place far away from where we lived and worked.

"Please don't phone me at home," he asked, early in our relationship. "I share a house with a friend, and although it's merely a convenient arrangement, she is a bit territorial."

I thought he was wonderful, and he made me feel good. After a few months of this relationship, I was getting very fond of him. As a Christian, I knew the relationship was neither clever nor right. And then (this is where Karin comes into the story), I went to a Christmas party and was enjoying chatting with various friends and colleagues when Karin called me to one side. With a look of sincere concern, she said that she understood that I was getting really close to Dr Ross Phillips; did I know he had a partner and was in a long term relationship? From my dumb reaction, she must have guessed that I didn't. She further enlightened me that he had left his wife for the girl he was now living with (once his nurse-secretary), and she was by no means 'just a good friend'. Quite frankly, I was angry, and I thought Karin was intrusive and interfering.

I went home stunned with this revelation. I felt chewed up and really hurt. After an unsettled weekend, I confronted my *darling* with the information from Karin, and he admitted that he had been *economical with the truth*. He had not wanted to mislead me but he was confused and torn between the stability of his long term relationship and me. He said he didn't want to lose me but was feeling bad about ditching his partner.

"My kids like her," he added weakly, "and I love her."

We broke up shortly after that. I was very heart-sore but a whole lot wiser. I had always felt a little miffed at Karin, but I know I should be hugely grateful to her. That was the year *before* I met and married Granville. Dr Phillips was Granville's doctor, so we have always had a delicate path to tread. Years after we were married, I told Granville.

Shortly after we arrived in England (and I was offered the real estate job), I contacted her to get some information regarding the property business. We soon became good friends, and although I still find her frankness startling, I know she is totally honest—a rare trait. Her husband is far more diplomatic but also very good company. One day I will tell my dear friend about the part she played in changing the direction of my life at that time. Today we enjoy the roast lamb and superb red wine Peter brought, eat lots of Easter chocolates, listen to classical music and relax.

22nd April

Today I bought a car. It's Granville's fault!

"Come on," he said, "you need a car. I just *cannot* see you driving my jalopy after swanking around in your Mercedes Benz."

He's right, but I am not ready to buy a car. I hate spending money. Especially big chunks of money! I'll go along to humour him.

First we went to a huge second-hand car yard with hundreds of cars. As we opened the door, a young salesman rushes out to 'claim us'.

"What a treat!" I whisper to Granville when the salesman went to get some forms from the office. "Here in England, the salesmen usually wait for you to beg for service before they get up from their chairs." I told the animated young chap what I wanted: silver or blue, leather seats, sky roof, air conditioning and good shape. He asked me about make and model. The poor boy was very confused when I told him that I didn't have a clue.

"Show me some shapes and colours…that's how I have bought all the cars I have ever owned. If I don't like the *look* of it, forget it."

He continued to protest that he couldn't possibly help me with so little to go on and looked imploringly at Granville, who just shrugged and followed me through the ocean of cars. There were hundreds. I chose a few that we liked and asked some questions…price, age, etc. We wanted to test drive three of the cars, which we did. In this particular company, test driving consisted of moving the vehicle slowly around the car lot.

"Thanks so much, but sorry, none of these cars feel right," I said as we leave a very frustrated car salesman scratching his head with his pencil.

We went off to another dealership to be told, "Sorry, we're going home. It's too quiet; we haven't had any customers today. We'll be open again on Tuesday."

I was tempted to say, "Hey, what am I? Chopped liver?"

We got a similar reception at two more garages. It may be that I was dressed too scruffy; it could also be that I am *female*.

Finally, on our way home through Weybridge, we spotted the Honda dealership and stopped to see what they had on their forecourt. There she was! I saw her before I had time to give the salesman my wish list. This enthusiastic chap took us on a fifteen mile (at least) trip—you could tell he loved his cars, and she was every bit as responsive and sleek on the road as I knew she would be. We drove back home with Granville beaming approval, his old workhorse clipping the hedges as we turned into our road.

The Tuesday after Easter, we packed up again to continue our travels, saying goodbye to Patrick, who had popped in for tea. I made him promise he would look after my garden—especially to water my new baby petunias. We have had loads of sunshine but absolutely no rain. It has been great to be able to touch base every four or five weeks. I am glad we have not let out our property. It is now off the agents' lettings books.

As we chug along the A23 towards the coast, I realise that we are streamlining the procedure of packing our goods, clothes and selves so that it takes no more than an hour from decision to take off. We now have much more space to move around than we had at the beginning of our sabbatical. By this, the third trip, we had thrown out even more of the unnecessary goods (including a Matthew Henry Bible Concordance which weighed 3 kg), a spare pup tent, a huge plastic container that looked like a coffin (strapped to the top of our vehicle—I have no idea what was in it) and 'emergency' equipment for every crisis imaginable. There was something that looked suspiciously like a spare engine too!

We parked again at Cooden, right on the pebbles. It's not an official campsite, so we were 'camping wild.' It's still unspoiled (relatively undiscovered)—a magical place with the sea so near you can park a few yards from the high tide line. That evening, we walked far along the beach towards Pevensey Bay, ducking under or jumping over the old, barnacle-encrusted wooden breakwaters. The tide was far out and the sunset beautiful enough to make me cry with thoughts of people with whom I wished could share the sunset too.

But the full impact of the loss and mind-blowing tragedy of Lucy's death came to me on one of my solo early morning walks along the beach. With a sharp clarity, I realized that since Lucy died I had not cried—shed tears—for her. In fact, as a kind of protective survival instinct, I had blocked my thoughts about her and contained them in small parcels, opening them briefly *only* when it was convenient.

That particular morning, the sea was slippery with millions of pale mauve shades (quite sombre). It had a timeless dimension, as if I was standing looking back at the past, letting it catch up with me. I closed my eyes and moving leisurely towards me came Lucy. Emotionally, I reached out to embrace her. I whispered into the soft morning air how much she meant to me, how much I missed her and what wonderful memories I had of her.

Lucy, I will never forget you—you are a part of my soul. I love you so very much.

Soon I was weeping, my shirt front sopping as I sobbed, taking in great gulps of air. It was a relief to allow myself to cry, remember her, and to feel the intensity of longing for her. I opened memory after memory, recalling years, days, and moments with her. I had not been able to do that before. I wrote this poem on her birthday a few months before our trip.

Lucy.

You are the warm place
I crawl to when I'm cold
An exclusive perfume;
My secret, sweet scented garden.

I experience colours, soft touches;
Can I hear you rustling nearby?
I love what you were and
Joy that you gave

But Lucy; I can't cry for you
If I let go - my soul will spill out.
I visit these memories for a moment
And walk away not looking back.

When I returned to the camper, Granville having prepared breakfast, my eyes were red and swollen, and for hours after crying, I felt exhausted, as if I had run a long, long way.

Later in the week, we return to the small campsite near the cliff at Seaford to top up our water supply, wash clothes and enjoy their super hot showers. After settling in, we take a long walk along the sea promenade, which stretches the full length of the town. A path continues over the steep cliffs that look over at Cookmere haven and the meandering river below. The hill rises almost vertically, with a golf course to our left and the sea far below to the right. One day, we watched as the golfers doing their casual golfer-walk and an old lady with a small dog crossed the hills on the far side of the Downs. The views out to sea and down to the winding river and estuary were spectacular.

On Thursday and Friday the weather was foul with rain and wind. It was interesting to watch people trapped in their caravans or campers. There is a strange guy who has a huge satellite dish attached to his camper. The blinds are always down

"He's a paedophile or mass murderer!" I tell Granville.

Our nearest neighbours are an elderly couple. She is large with long grey hair usually tied back; he is even larger with back bent as if by years of hard work. He lovingly helps her out and tucks her back into the camper each time she goes in and out. Earlier, when the rain was pouring down, he ran out to meet her with an umbrella. I can see he adores her. Her name is Mavis, but she is very quiet—I have not heard her call out his name. Adjacent are a sour-faced couple. She works like a slave, and he drinks beer. I see him walk to the ablutions now and again. She does the really heavy stuff: emptying the waste water, putting up the tent, and I saw her changing a tire on the car. He's a lazy sod—doesn't lift a finger. When he talks to her, he shouts; swears too. She looks really downtrodden. Some campers seem to hibernate and quietly carry on with whatever they are doing.

"The couple in site twenty-four are planning a robbery," I inform Granville.

He says my imagination is getting the better of me.

"But I saw them with plans of a building, and I am sure it's a bank."

"Good grief, woman, don't be stupid," he says heading for the beach with his fishing rod.

"You'll catch your death in that horrible weather," I shouted at his retreating back.

I didn't catch his reply, but I know it was sarcastic.

I read a few chapters of my Francine Rivers novel and crocheted more of the squares for Gregory's blanket. Looking out of the window, I noticed that the wild bunnies did not seem to be put off by the rain as they scampered around, digging here and there and nibbling the grass. That evening, I put on my raincoat and walked along the seafront just to get out of the camper for a while, taking my mobile phone so that I can answer some of the texts from Susan: *Where are the old mandates filed? What was the name of the guy who was interested in buying Squirrel Woods? Where are the instructions for mail-merge?*

The next morning was Saturday, and we moved the camper back to Cooden Beach. The sun came out as we backed onto the shingle, and although there was a breeze, it was lovely. The sea was brown and choppy from the rain of the past few days. We get a call from Allan, who was coming to see us and bringing our friend, Lois Levine. How we met Lois is a strange story. I was sitting in my office at Global Real Estate in January 2001 on a dull Saturday morning. A clear South African voice on the phone said, "Hi there, this is Lois Levine. I have just arrived from South Africa!"

I would never have guessed!!

"I am looking for a flat to rent."

"Hello, Lois," I replied, "what's your budget?"

"About £50 per week," she replied.

At that time, the average one bedroom flat in the area was in the region of £250 per week!

"Now listen, Lois, get on a train and come for coffee! I will pick you up at Guildford station, and we can talk, but I must be honest— there is no way you will find anything to rent at £50 per week…a room perhaps, but not a flat. But I would love to meet you and will try to help you in any way I can."

Well…that was the beginning of a great friendship. Lois has been an amazing influence in our lives. She lives, breathes, and carries around with her the love of Jesus. It shows in her walk her talk and the joy she spreads. She met Allan soon after she arrived and asked him to join her in finding a church, and the story continues on to much happiness and many times of burning the midnight oil as they argued about God and Jesus. Then Allan accepted Jesus as his Saviour. I had prayed since Allan was born that he would come to realise the power and love of God through Jesus, his Son.

Back to our day in the camper at Cooden Beach with Allan and Lois. Granville did a wonderful tuna salad with nuts and apple, and we sat around the small table in the camper, drinking coke and wine—simply enjoying the day. Later, we walked along the beach, paddling and skimming stones. It was low tide, and the sand went out for many yards. We love sharing our beach with others. They left us to go back to Surrey just as the sky was putting on its show of soft pink sundowner colours.

The next day, Sunday, the beach was bouncing with weekenders: the bathers, fishermen, jet skis and windsurfers making the whole scene like a brochure for weekend breaks at the seaside. We decided to return home after lunch. The garden was a glorious riot of colour from the petunias, pansies, roses, shrubs and the bright green grass. Again, it was great to bath, wash clothes and change bed linen.

It's quite funny; you know how our adult kids find it amazing that we, as oldies, can find one another remotely sexy. Our children are no exception. The next day, Granville and I were changing the bed linen, and whilst tucking the duvets in their covers and pulling fitted sheets over the mattress, there were grunts and noises:

"Hey, push your bit in a bit…no that's not enough…now shake it well…that's right…bit more. Stop! That's too much…fiddle inside and see what has happened."

We were concentrating on the task at hand.

"Now work fast and tuck your bit in. No, no, no how many times have I told you? You must start with it inside out…otherwise it's much harder? Now start again, or it will never shake down to get to the right bits. Actually, Granville, you go away…it works better when I do it alone!" I added.

At that point, I heard the back door sliding closed. I ran to the window to see Patrick disappearing out the back gate. The next time we met him, there was no mention of our bedroom antics, but I think he is now seriously confused about what we get up to.

28th April

We collected my new car. We drove around to show it to Patrick, and he said, "Nice wheels, Anne!"

I called in to see Allan at his home in the centre of town. First he admires the car then he asks me to take him grocery shopping. We often need to help him with shopping and lifts because he only has a motor bike not suitable for conveying bags of groceries. It's a huge, powerful and horrible animal. I pray lots that he doesn't get squashed by a bus or something awful. I try to *not* worry about it. As we roam around Tesco and he casually throws his purchases into the trolley, we talk about his work and his future.

"My love, you must decide what you want to do. If you feel you want to break out and do something else, go for it." (He says he is wondering whether he should study for his teacher's diploma.)

It's a joy to spend time with him; he is easy to be with. When we arrived in England in 1997 and for the first time since he was born, I had him all to myself. It's strange how you can be around your children but be too busy to really discern their feelings or understand what is going on in their heads. Spending time, especially alone with your children, is precious, valuable time. There will always be things to do—washing, chores and phone-call distractions—but those times (could be just a moment) when we can connect, share, talk and look one another in the eye may not come again. Miss that opportunity, and it's gone forever: irretrievable!

Allan shared his new found joy in finding Jesus—the peace and contentment of realising God loves and cares for him and wants the best in his life. As I drive back home after dropping him and his groceries on the doorstep of his apartment, I pray

"Lord, now he needs a wife. Please find him someone nice."

On the way back home, I pass Global Real Estate.

Hey...I have stopped worrying about the office all the time. I have finally started to really relax. But the umbilical cord is still intact. Am I going to find it hard to pick up the reins and carry on at the end of our sabbatical? How difficult will it be to

go back to being controlled every day by the whole package of obligations?

I push the questions well back in my mind.

5

The Obby Oss

On the last day of April, Granville wanted to get back on the road in the camper; our next trip was to Cornwall. After he had been to the health clinic for what we call 'blood letting' (he is being constantly monitored after a twelve-clot embolism from which he amazingly recovered), we set off for Padstow, a fishing village recently made even more popular by the chef Rick Stein.

We arrived at the campsite, which was in some fields above the town. The weather had been mad. In the space of a few hours, we had blue sky, drizzle, torrential rain and even some hail. In fact, typically English weather. By the time we had finished our dinner, it was too late to walk into the village, so we talked to various fellow campers. They told us that there was a special May Day parade the next day, so we decided to drive into Padstow early and have breakfast on the quayside to be ready to enjoy the activities.

1st May: Spring Day
It was a day of magic and wonder that will live long in my memory. We drove down to the quiet little village at about 7 a.m. in the morning and enjoyed a breakfast of bacon and eggs with hot buttered toast. The smells mingled with the salty scents of sea,

harbour and fresh paint. Bobbing fishing boats created a picturesque, busy backdrop. Then we watched as the town slowly came to life. We had no idea of what to expect, not really understanding what everyone was so busy doing. By 9.30 a.m., there were crowds—tourists and indigenous—many in strange costume. Soon every street, square and pavement right up to the harbour was alive with hundreds of people. The harbour boats fluttered with colourful flags, tea rooms and restaurants were decorated with 'Obby Oss' and May Day garlands and some shops and newsagents were selling mementos and playing delightful folk music.

Many revellers were dressed in traditional costumes of white with a blue or red sash tied around the middle and a checked blue or red neck scarf, rather like the Morris dancers we had seen before in other parts of England. Some had ribbons and rings of spring flowers or leaves in their hair; some wore straw hats.

We shuffled along with the throng, and then, around mid morning, the 'Obby Oss' made its appearance to much shouting, dancing, stick and drum banging. It swirled and twirled and wove its way through as the crowds parted. This weird costumed creature (a local man dressed up) was swathed in a black cape and wore a pointed witches' hat which came right down over his face: a scary face with painted red teeth and evil eyes. It was followed all through the town, up and down the streets by the drummers, dancers, singers and pipers. They chanted a repetitive song with a haunting simple tune as they jostled along the narrow, crowded streets. The atmosphere was thrilling.

A Mayople stood in a small square around which young girls danced. Bunting and flags hung over cobbled streets filled with the aroma of pastries, fish, chips and coffee. We discovered that these May Day celebrations dated back to the 13th century, and that this was a pagan festival to welcome the spring. The 'Obby Oss' was 'searching for maidens to capture to promote and ensure the blessing of fertility'. We were told at least six different stories of the origins of the 'Obby Oss' from the six people we asked. This was the most important day of the year in this charming fishing community. How fortunate to be there at that special time, to be spectators to the colourful traditions of the hugely enjoyable tradition. One old chap told us in a hushed hissing voice that it was an evil pagan festival. Anyway, evil or not, we enjoyed the fun and silliness of it all, and many hundreds did too. The fun and frivolities continued on and on. The weather was wonderful, and spring well and truly welcomed! We looked back at a bouncing, colourful, happy scene as we left to have lunch in a quieter spot.

Now as I sit in the camper writing up my diary, it is late afternoon. There is yet another special scene in front of us. We are parked on the beach at a cosy little cove—Trevone Bay. The sky and the sea are many shades of blue and green, the horizon is dark viridian touched with ultramarine. Nearer us, the sea is a washy turquoise. The green hills and craggy cliffs around us frame the soft, sandy beach where two young people in wheelchairs are having a race. It must be tough going on the sand, as their minders—tanned young guys—have a great time shouting as they push their seated friends. To the far right against the rocks is a family with small children. They have stripped and are running in all directions, their pink little bodies a strange sight in this paedophilic obsessed country. How wonderful that they and their mommies feel free enough to enjoy the sun and the sea with such innocent joy. Years ago, kids were so safe that one never even entertained the thought that people would want to harm them or think strange and warped thoughts. Until I arrived in England, I did not know what a paedophile was.

About an hour ago, there was an air display by the Red Arrows. The magnificent little jets were zapping around the sky in perfect unison, changing from arrow formation to birds-in-flight, from tight knots then to a diamond shape. Those boys must have nerves of steel. They splayed out in several directions, re-grouped, flew frighteningly low and left trails of coloured smoke in the sky—red, white and blue. To see the air display in this setting—over the sea and hills around—was so exciting. We guessed that the display must have had something to do with the May Day celebrations.

I thanked God for the privilege of being alive, of being aware and existing. Always, when I have the reality of being alive with a sharp state of feeling (feeling both pain and incredible joy), I miss my beautiful Lucy more acutely than ever. I closed my eyes.

I saw her in the swirling crowd…lovely…laughing and pulling funny faces. She is dancing around that maypole with flowers in her long red and ringlet-curly hair, her white diaphanous dress swirling. I can hear her singing in her deep completely off-key voice—living the happiness. It was as if she treasured each moment when she was here with us. Did she know she had so little time?

2nd May

We drove along the coast to Newquay. I remembered it from long ago when I first visited England as teenager. My recollections were of a small, cute seaside town but today all we find is a noisy, smelly, garish place. Now commercialised to a sickening degree, there are horrible games arcades, surf shops, cheap penny shops and bed-and-breakfasts offering rooms for £15 per night. I feel it has taken on the air of a rather seedy seaside town. We returned to the camper and hurried off along the coast through small towns and sandy surfing beaches—their long unbroken rollers slowly arriving on the shore. We called in at two and watched surfers from all over the world but mainly from South Africa and Australia. Their 'kombi' and other camper vehicles, which were plastered with stickers, indicated their origins.

"I want to go back into Padstow," I said suddenly. "Many of the little shops and art galleries were shut for the festival. They looked interesting. Do you mind, Love?"

We returned to a much quieter town. In fact, it seemed a little tired and sleepy. I wandered up and down the cobbled streets, happily enjoying the shops. The antique shops, art galleries filled with paintings of boats and the sea, and the kitchenware shops occupied me for hours as I browsed and stopped to buy small gifts and postcards to send to friends and family. I found an amazing shop that was selling fresh fish. I rushed back to tell Granville, who was writing in the camper. Eyes aglow, he set off and returned later laden with several white paper carrier bags.

We went back to the little Trevone Bay to enjoy our fishy lunch, looking out over a drizzly scene. After a post-lunch nap, with Classic FM lulling us into a stupor, we took advantage of the break in the weather and climbed up the grassy hill to walk along the cliff edge. The views over the sea to the far bays and towns tucked into the coastline were picture-postcard, as were the fields of wild flowers on the cliffs and the stone walls. Granville was terrified I would get blown off the cliff every time I went within five yards of the edge. He is such a caring, darling man.

It would take a hurricane to propel my ninety kilograms off any precipice.

4th May

Today we investigated two towns that our friends Karin and Peter had told us about: Rock and Polzeath. Granville was a little reluctant, but I felt it would be worth the trip, so off we went. Rock seemed a bit boring—a small yachting village and not much else (unless we missed something). We continued on to Polzeath and parked the camper on the flat, sandy beach.

What a beautiful place!

There were crowds of bathers, surfers and paddlers. Small children were building sandcastles, and many young and old took advantage of the wind which came up later to fly a variety of kites. Later we ate our yummy lunch of seafood bought at the Rick Stein shop in Padstow. (Shrimps, stuffed crab, salmon pate and garlic olives).

That evening when we returned to the campsite, we realise we should be heading back towards home. We have a dinner date with friends on the 9th, and before we left on this leg of our trip, we had booked a trip to South Africa flying out on the 12th May. Allan is accompanying us on our trip back home next month. It will be his first trip back since we came to England in 1996. I wonder what he will make of all the changes. And wow…South Africa has changed *so much* in the past six years.

On the way back home, we visited a National Trust property— Castle Drago. This creation was the combined inspiration of Edwin Lutyens, the renowned architect, and Julius Drewe, a rich business man. It was built between 1911 and 1933 of solid granite and is a masterpiece. It's said to be the last true castle built in the British Isles. We twist through narrow roads and the charming 'roses-around-the-door' villages, heading for home.

Back home it's sorting, washing and packing for our trip 'home' to South Africa. We had a lovely supper with Tosca and Luke Cominelli who bought a house through me last year. One of the advantages I have always enjoyed in the property industry is that clients often become friends. As a matter of fact, Granville was a client to whom I sold a house, but that's a long story! As we enjoy the juicy steaks prepared and braaied (barbecued) by Luke, we recall how, shortly after they had bought their superb home in one of Ascot's best areas, it was totally flooded. Before they moved into the house, they went to Europe for three weeks, and whilst they were away, thousands of litres of water poured into the house from a broken pipe in the ceiling. The deluge met them before they opened the front door: the interior of the house was completely ruined. It took six months of drying out, rebuilding and repairs before they could occupy their home. At first, they were devastated, but the insurance cover enabled them to renovate and restore the house as they wanted and exactly to their taste. They had done a marvellous job. It was stunning. They asked me how I was going to cope with getting back to work after having a long break.

"With great difficultly," I replied.

10th May

Today is Granville's sixty-ninth birthday. Gregory, Patty, Patrick, Maxine and Allan come around for a braai. They bring presents and rude cards. It was warm and sunny—amazing weather for England.

I guess soon the weather fundis (experts) will be saying that there is a drought. Confusing place, England! It rains for months, and then, after just a few weeks of sunshine, there are water shortages.

As we sit around the patio table, I bet Granville £70 that he could not keep out of the shops for three days. My bet was badly worded. "I bet you will be *in your car* and down at the supermarket within hours."

"You're on," he said.

My man is a total shopaholic! He loves to shop! Anticipating a trip to the shops, his eyes brighten, his step quickens, and he comes alive. The actual experience is a joy and delight to him, and he savours the entire process. In a supermarket, he always starts off with a basket.

"Not much to buy today," he'll say, bouncing towards the supermarket bakery. "Just bread and croissants! Wait a minute...don't we need apples? And washing powder?"

He usually changes to a trolley when the basket is spilling over the edges and the handle is cutting his fingers in two. If an item or article is labelled *Bargain*, *New Low Price*, or *Two for the Price of One*, he is a lost soul. Even if he does not have any use for the offered article, foodstuff or whatever…he will still buy it! Our store cupboards are evidence of his weakness, as are my generous proportions!!

So, the crafty old bugger won the bet by *not getting into his car* for three days to shop. He did all the shopping on foot. It did limit him to some extent, but he managed. The hernia in his groin and backache he incurred were his wages for being so cunning. I was as mad as a snake to part with £70.

6

South Africa My Home

11th May

It's the Sunday before our trip to South Africa. Today is a special day of thanksgiving. Prayers I had prayed for many years were answered. At Allan's full-immersion baptism at Holy Trinity (Brompton) in London, he confirmed his acceptance of Jesus as his Lord and Saviour. When my babies were born, I dedicated them to God. The baptism service was joy to my heart. Allan chose a long, long drug-hazed route but a few months ago had a real experience with the Lord after doing an Alpha course. Lucy was safe with Jesus, and it was with relief that I now knew where Allan would be too when he died. One day, a few months after Lucy died, Allan asked me, "Mom, do you still miss Lucy so much?

I thought and then said what was in my heart.

"Allan…when Lucy died, I was very, very sad. The pain and the missing her has not gone away, but if you had been the one to die…I would be totally broken. I know where Lucy is, and I have peace. If you died right now, I would not have that same peace. I would not know where you were."

12th May

We did some final packing and shopping for our trip to South Africa and then were off to the airport. The check-in was tedious, but the plane was virtually empty, so the eleven hour trip was a little easier. The next day, we were very late disembarking in Johannesburg: we had to run across from the International airport to the Internal Flights section to get our connection to Durban. Breathing heavily as I pushed our mountainous trolley, I hoped the gifts that made my luggage twenty kilograms overweight would be appreciated by friends and family.

Kate and Bill (my sister and brother-in-law) were waiting for us at Durban Airport. It's great to see them again—I always cry with joy. They are solid, reliable, trustworthy, and dependable. I love them. Granville was nervous of my family when we were first married; he thought they were far too outspoken and intimidating, but now he too had grown to love them all. My sister (we were a family of two girls) is the most precious person. I see so much of my mum in her: straight, direct, funny and totally honest. Often my teenage toes would be scrunched up with embarrassment as mother turned to my friends and said things like, "You've got a lovely skin dear…but you should get rid of a bit of weight, or you will be the size of a house after you've had babies." And to my Afrikaans friend Sarie, "Now don't you teach Annie to speak your language—I don't want her speaking with an Afrikaans accent. It's bad enough that she has to learn it at school. Don't this Nationalist government realise that this is Natal, not the Transvaal, Sarie dear?"

Now, please, don't deduce from these revelations that mom was nasty. She was the kindest, most generous woman you could ever wish to meet. We can only think that she lacked the programme that deciphered between candid and offensive comments. Amazingly, people of all ages were drawn to her, and when we were growing up, our home was always heaving with visitors and stay-over guests.

It's just the same with Kate. She has a heart of gold, but my mom's lack of tact is definitely genetic.

"Hi!" Kate greets us with squeezes and hugs. "Hey, you guys are blossoming. Granville, the gypsy life must suit you." Turning to Allan, "Wow…you look smart, all cleaned up. What happened to the hippy with dread-locks?" And then she called to Bill, who was waiting to greet us, "Come on, Bill, grab that bag from Granville. He's a *moeg ou toppie* (tired old chap)."

The drive up the N3 freeway to Pietermaritzburg (where Kate and Bill live) takes us approximately 45 minutes. Sights that remind me that I am no longer in England have immediate impact: children herding two skinny cows across a four-lane highway, women with stacks of firewood on their heads walking gracefully along the side in the recovery lane, an old car dented and battered, coughing black smoke, holds up a 2003 Mercedes Benz in the fast lane.

We are home! This is Africa, and it's good to be back.

When we arrived at Kate and Bill's townhouse, we unpacked our bags and striped off several layers of clothes. Although it was autumn in Kwa Zulu Natal, it was several degrees higher than the English spring weather we had left behind. We enjoyed a cup of tea, home-made shortbread and talked about all sorts of general family things in light shorthand, laughing and relaxed in each other's company. Later, we went to a large shopping centre where there was a Spur Steakhouse. As Bill parks the car, Allan asked, "Uncle Bill, what are all these guys doing buzzing around the car park with *Car Guard* written all over their shirts?"

"They're here to look after your car! You pay them anything from 50c to R2 to guard your car from thieves and hijackers. Since introducing the system, the car theft and car crime figures have dropped significantly."

"Shucks!" said Allan looking worried.

The evening is fun, easy and relaxed. Ryan, Kate's eldest son, and his wife Elizabeth are there to greet us. They look marvellous. Tough, tanned Ryan (35), is a mountain of a man…a farmer and full of fun. He was my mom's favourite grandchild, and I can understand why. Elizabeth is good-looking but not in a fussy, girly way. She has clear skin, and a bright and intelligent face with the calm resilience she will need to cope with life as a farmer's wife. She is a school teacher, an excellent sportswoman (hockey, I think), and has loved Ryan since she was a schoolgirl.

We enjoy Ryan's off-beat humour, and soon we are hearing about incidents on the farm that probably wouldn't sound particularly funny unless you have lived in Africa. We had a great supper of huge juicy steaks. There was so much to talk about, catching up on what each one had been doing.

As we were lingering over our coffees, the conversation turned to Mom and Dad then to Dad's complicated Last Will & Testament. Ryan had worked on Dad's farm since he left school, but he lived a few miles away in Mooi River in a flat that Mom had bought for him. Two weeks after Mom's funeral, Ryan moved into the large farmhouse to look after Dad and help with the running of the dairy and timber farm.

Dad suffered brain damage when he had stroke at the time of Mom's death. He'd been at Mom's bedside for days but had left to go back to the farm to have a bath and generally to attend to matters. Soon after he got home, the hospital phoned to say Mom had taken a turn for the worst. He rushed out of the house and drove like a maniac back to her hospital bedside, but when he got there, she was covered with a sheet. He had such a huge shock he collapsed with a massive heart attack by her bedside. The doctor, who had been called to certify that Mom was dead, had to administer emergency treatment to Dad. He was admitted and was so ill that for days he didn't know what was happening or that his beloved Flo was dead.

His recovery was slow, but the boys were wonderful. They

cooked his meals, helped him to rehabilitate from the stroke, drove him around and generally cared for the whole of Dad's private and business affairs. Dad missed Mom so much and was grieving to the point of selfish indulgence. Nothing and no-one else mattered: his life and his pain were all he could think about. Mom and Dad had been together since she was thirteen and he was fifteen. He was helpless without her; she even chose the clothes he was to wear each day, putting them out on the bed for him.

Like many men of his generation, he couldn't cook, clean or keep house. He never fully recovered from the stroke. He became a very different man from the strong, straight-laced business-man farmer and church leader than he had been before it all happened. Then later in the year during which mom died, he married again. Suzanna, an elegant woman of about fifty, happened to be visiting her son (a young man who farmed nearby) when they told her about Dad and how lonely he was.

One evening in July, he phoned to say that he had a surprise for me. He sounded happy. He handed the phone over to Suzanna, and this syrupy-sweet voice came over the phone, and in short, what she said was that she and dad were getting married in two weeks' time; she said that she was *not* after his money (she had her own income) and that he was such a darling man she just wanted to look after him.

What a joke!

Initially, I was happy for him. I felt relieved that he had found someone to be with him, although it did all seem rather soon after mom's death. He was so very lost, and his mind was wandering. But the attractive woman he married just ten months after mom died slowly and surely alienated the family from Dad. She told dad that the family were stealing from him and causing trouble. She told Ryan to leave and that his grandpa didn't need him any more. Ryan was devastated. He had worked on the farm for years; even before he left school, he helped with the running of the business and the farm.

Since leaving school and agricultural college, it was now his full time occupation.

Dad's new wife also prevented Bill and Kate from seeing him. They were frantically worried about him but just couldn't get to speak to him alone to find out if he was happy. Then she badgered him until he changed his Will. There are no prizes for guessing in whose favour! The area where Dad lived was really small town, so the information came filtering back to us from many sources: African maids (always a wonderful source of information), farm labourers, lawyer's secretaries, estate agents, hairdressers, old friends and neighbours. They were appalled and amazed at the changes that were happening, but Dad was in no state to take charge.

As time passed, Kate said that she and the boys thought Dad was terrified of Suzanna. She carried out the whole operation in the most diabolical way—but with sweetness and smiles. Someone reported that she said she was only doing the best for the old man, and that all he needed was peace and quiet without the interference of his family. She was very plausible, and he called her his Angel. She took charge of everything. Within a year, we all realised that she had achieved total control.

We tried through several channels to get help for him, but it was extremely difficult. After they married, she would always phone me first to say that Dad wanted a word with me. When he spoke to me, she seemed to be right there. Soon, she refused to allow Dad to see any of the family at all, and whenever I phoned he was always 'sleeping' or 'up at the cow shed'. He called me less and less as time passed until his calls petered out totally. I was very worried.

The Christmas before Dad died, I had made a special trip to South Africa to see him. I had not been able to speak to him on the phone for months, and there were bizarre reports not only from the immediate family but also from neighbours, who had taken the trouble to phone me in England. Several stories were so shocking I thought they may have been exaggerated. Comments came via the very effective local grapevine:

"He looks very ill and getting thinner every time I see him"

"Phew…the *baas*…he is too sick…ow, ow too bad."

"Your father looks very ill…a shadow of the big man we knew."

I was determined to visit the farm as soon as we arrived in South Africa. Using Kate's mobile phone, I called the farm from Durban airport to say that we had landed, and we were on our way to see Dad. Suzanna, in a rather panicky voice, responded, "No, you can't come now."

"Why? Can I speak to the old man?" I asked.

"Sorry, he is busy, and anyway, we are just leaving for Johannesburg. Then we will be away until after Christmas. What a pity we'll miss you!" she added quickly.

Granville was seriously worried and insisted, "Bill, head towards the farm. We're going there *now* whatever that woman says!"

Two hours later, we arrived unexpectedly on the farm; Dad heard the car coming up the dirt track and ran out. He was surprised to see us. Although he was distressed and confused, he repeated over and over how happy he was to see us.

"Kate and Bill never visit me," he said sadly.

When I told him that his wife obstructed their visits, he suddenly stiffened and, with fear in his eyes, whispered, "You shouldn't have come…she doesn't like me to mix with the family; she doesn't like the family to come here."

"Dad, I have come five thousand miles to see you. We love you and are very worried about you."

He cried and so did I. He was dead within six months.

13th May

It was wonderful to wake in Africa that morning. Bird calls welcomed us to a new day. When I got up to make the early morning tea, there were the special smells of wood-smoke, grasses and dry earth.

I love the autumn weather in Kwa Zulu Natal. There's usually very little rain, and the skies are clear, intense blue. The days are mild and thoroughly enjoyable.

Kate and Bill have lived in Pietermaritzburg for many years. 'Maritzburg, as it is known, is a small city about 80 kilometres from Durban and was for many years the administrative capital of the Province of Natal. After Zululand was incorporated into Natal a decade ago, the province was renamed Kwa Zulu Natal. This beautiful 'Old Natal' area is known as 'the last outpost of the British Empire'. In the mid 1800s, the area was settled by immigrants from England. The plum-in-the-mouth accents of the white people living here are similar to the 'Queen's English', as people used to call it, and many of the older folk still refer to England as 'the Old Country'.

The plan of action for that day was that I should get an appointment with the executor of Dad's Will. We called at their offices in the city. When finally I got to speak to the clerk handing the file on behalf of the solicitor, she was obstructive and rude. We left the office feeling frustrated and annoyed. We had no idea who was living on the farm, and what had happened to Dad's timber business and his other properties. The family solicitor and firm of accountants, who had handled Mom's and Dad's affairs for many years, had been dismissed six months before Dad died. Then we discovered that some long lost cousins (who had now unfortunately appeared) had moved into the manager's cottage on the farm 'to help Aunty Suzanna'. We decided to pay them a visit later that afternoon.

The long-lost-and-now-unfortunately-found cousins were sly-eyed and guarded. We were sad to see the place taken over and controlled by virtual strangers. *They* were running the farm and timber business. My dad's widow met us at the gate of the main farmhouse with a face like thunder. She was *not* happy to see us. We asked questions regarding the farm and estate, but she just shrugged and replied in a pathetic voice, "I don't know a thing. Ask the solicitors."

Then she rambled on distractedly about having so much to do…and things were in such mess…being confused, not knowing what to do. She added that the (long-lost-and-now-unfortunately-found) cousins, who had appeared when Dad was ill, were helping her 'sort everything out'.

Kate, Bill, Granville and I got back into the car feeling heavy with helplessness. We drove back down the dusty road to 'Maritzburg discussing the whole mad affair. We were appalled that we could not get clarity from anyone at the lawyer's office or from the accountants. When we phoned we were fobbed off with, "Sorry, your Dad's next of kin is Suzanna Goldstone. We cannot discuss anything with you."

The more we heard, the more we were determined to get an appointment to see the executor of Dad's Will. After waiting for over an hour (even with a booked appointment), we were ushered into his office. He didn't seem to know what was going on either! We asked him if the farm was on the sales market!

He said, "No." (We had seen it advertised by a company specialising in farm properties who had confirmed that they had a mandate from Mrs Goldstone and her solicitor).

We asked him what had been removed from the farm. He said that nothing had been removed, but we knew from the farm workers and house girls that the farmhouse was devoid of all the old furniture. A farm-hand told us that the tractors and irrigation equipment had gone to 'the baas over the hill', (Suzanna's son who farmed only a few miles away).

That evening, we had a family gathering to assess the situation. After hours of discussion and many cups of tea and coffee, we unanimously decided that it was best to let matters be—at least for the time being. We felt that contesting the will would cause us more angst and bitterness, and there was no guarantee that we would win at litigation. We also heard that the cousins were now fighting with Suzanna because she had promised them tenancy for life, and they did not realise that she was going to sell the farm.

Early the next morning, when the grass was still wet, we went out once more to say our goodbyes to the farm. We parked the car on the dirt road leading up to the farm and walked up to the top of the hill from where we had a view over the whole farm, the mountain and beyond. It was a clear still day.

To our left was the Kudu—the little mountain with dark green forests at its feet and soft beige grass on the foothills and summit. Paths criss-crossed to the huts down in the valley where many of the farm workers stayed. We could see them coming and going. Directly below us were the unpainted, galvanised tin-roofs of the farmhouse, cowsheds, and timber drying sheds, to the left of that, the farm manager's cottage. So many parts of the patchwork below us made up the whole quilt of our memories: water tanks, the chicken runs (now empty), bales of hay stacked against the breeze block walls of the compound, the brown water of the dam, the old rowing boat floating near the small sandy edge. Just down from the lower farm boundary were the neighbour's citrus orchards. Ahead, far in the distance, was Edendale township, where thousands of black families still lived clustered together in their tiny homes as allocated to them by the Nationalist government planners during the establishment of *group areas* or *separate development,* both euphemistic terms for apartheid.

As we stood there on that hill, Allan was recalling his adventures on the farm—wonderful times that he'd spent with Lucy and his cousins, Ryan, Helen and Llewellyn. Many incidents came into Allan's mind: running from wild bees after he and Llewellyn had disturbed a hive to steal honey, horror as a six foot mamba waved above them in a tree, playing with the little black children in their mud huts, letting out the chickens from the fowl-run, and Lucy and Helen ('the girls') telling tales on them. They would go down to the dam to swim, fish or just wallow like hippos in the mud. Once Ryan got a fish hook stuck into his hand, and he needed surgery to remove it.

"When we came back to the farmhouse covered in mud, Gran would joke that she wasn't sure if we were little *umfaans* (black boys) or her boys! She would put us all in the huge bath, fill it with bubbles and scrub us clean. Yus, Auntie Kate, it's a wonder us boys have any family jewels left, the way she sent that scrubbing brush around our private parts!"

I left the little group laughing at these recollections and continued down the path to the manager's cottage. When Lucy and Allan were small, my then-husband and I moved onto the farm, having built this house up the hill from the main farmhouse. Lucy was a podgy four-year-old and 'her' baby (Allan, who she called 'Bub') was just over a year old. She adored him. As soon as he could walk, she would lead him over to Granny's house as early in the morning as I would allow.

The two little figures are walking away from me. He toddling, falling often, and she holding his hand possessively, helping him up, dusting him down, picking off the dry grass from his babygro. Lucy...talking all the while. Their ginger and white-blond heads disappearing over the hill.

When Kate joined me, we were both very quiet, just standing there for a while. It was a very painful episode for us both. There was too much to say. There were movies playing reel after reel in our minds' cinema. We continued down hill to the dam and through the small wooded area, remembering the great times we all had there, Mom and Dad and their open-hearted generosity.

Saying goodbye to the farm was not easy. Looking back at the tin roofs of the farmhouse and buildings for the last time, Kate and I said, almost in unison, "Life's not fair!"

Several days later, we started talking about our memories—the life and lives that were part of the family farm Kudu Hills. (A Kudu is a large antelope). Kate recalled the amazing curries Mom made (real Indian curry that blew your head off), and her disgustingly weak tea. Her tea was famous far and wide. She used one tea bag in a six cup pot of tea! The moment she heard a car or truck coming up to the farm, she would rush out to invite the occupants to tea/breakfast/lunch/dinner dependant upon the time of day. She was hugely hospitable. At her funeral, one of the local sugar farmers, after offering his condolences, asked me, "Can I tell you a secret? Flo Goldstone's tea was legendary! It was as weak as piddle. All of us farmers who were regular visitors to your mom and dad carried extra teabags in our pockets to slip into the cup when she wasn't looking."

Mom had very poor eyesight so would never have known. I am sure even the visiting Christian missionaries from the UK, who often spent time on the farm with Mom and Dad, must also have felt that they needed to add an extra teabag or two to the pot!!

Funny thing. Today as I write, the lawyers have e-mailed to say that the farm had been sold, so now we can never go back except in memories. This was a bad situation, a great injustice. We'll probably never have any idea of just how bad or how unjust—we didn't dwell on it. We knew that it would do us more harm if we allowed the venom of anger to infect us.

A few days after our visit to the farm, as we were preparing for a weekend away, I got a call from the Global office. It took me instantly back to the day-to-day, dog-eats-dog world of business. The rush, rush, rush and 'it must be done *now*' attitude was tangible, even from five thousand miles away. They were having a problem with a vendor who would only deal with me. When she was told that I was in South Africa, she got really angry, so I rang her. An hour and several expensive calls to England later, the problem was finally sorted and the client pacified. When I called Global to report back,

I could tell they were involved in the next drama—their call to me a tiny part of a hugely frantic busy day of making a living.

"Whoa! It's not going to be easy to go back to all that stuff," I announced to Granville, Kate, Bill and Allan, who had been waiting patiently for me to finish the business calls.

The weekend bags were packed into the car, and we set off to do the Midlands Meander. First stop was Howick Falls, a journey of about ten kilometres into marvellous *krantz* (mountain) scenery. The falls are impressive! The water drops hundreds of metres into the river below. Nearby are curio, indigenous arts, craft shops and a tea room in an old house that served the biggest slice of delicious, moist carrot-cake I have ever tasted.

Then Kate took us to a fantastic shop: Tabo's Antiques. Tabo is an enterprising young man who has set up a very lucrative trade in old furniture. He goes into the Zulu villages, locations and townships with a truck-load of new furniture. It is modern, smart, and new. He trades it for old pieces that the Africans have tucked away in their little huts and homes, and often, he told us, he has found them in the cowsheds and chicken runs. He restores or fixes the items and sells them in his shop. Some are really wonderful pieces: *Africana*, Victorian English and early 18th-century Dutch furniture standing peacefully side by side.

There is also a fantastic weaving shop in Howick. They sell hand woven mohair and wool carpets and other woven goods. The place is run by a young chap who provides an outlet for the Zulu ladies (many of them poor and illiterate) to bring their work. He provides the wool and the shop front to display their work. They take commissions for individual designs too. We bought a super runner rug with a very simple geometric design in brown, cream and black. These touches of Africa really give one a joyful lift on a dark winter's day in England.

Allan was very excited to be back in Africa after such a long time away. He bought a lot of African curios—I had no idea how he was going to get them all back home! Later over lunch, Bill asked Allan for his thoughts on being back home. I was reminded of the many times when a celebrity, visiting South Africa for the first time, was asked almost the same question by reporters at the airport on *entering* the country,

"What do you think of South Africa?"

"Uncle Bill, I am still trying to take it all in. There are huge changes."

We continue on our way, the weather beautiful: blue, blue sky, the drying grass a soft butter yellow colour and the trees a myriad of autumn hues. Allan called for Bill to stop the car several times so that he could photograph the people and the uniquely African scenes— *Rondavel* dwellings (round thatch huts), skinny stripy cows, dry *meilie* (corn) fields and two small black barefoot children in khaki shorts and thin holey grey pullovers and big smiles. I had forgotten how special these children are. They have so little, yet they have ready smiles and bright, inquisitive eyes. We passed women with various loads smoothly balanced on their heads: sticks, water drums and even once a chest of drawers.

One photo-stop had us all saying, "Wow…isn't that amazing!"

On the way to Lion's River, there was a mountain rising steeply from a lake. The mountain itself, the orange and brown trees and dry grass, and the sky all reflected with mirror-clarity in the still water. Then as we watched, a duck landed on the water, cutting across the duplicate image. In its wake, soft ripples distorted the reflection until they faded out to the banks on the far side.

We stopped for lunch at Happy Hill Guest Farm. While the men were tucking into huge homemade apple pie and cream at the end of the meal, Kate and I went to see what the facilities and bedrooms were like. Kate asked one of the black girls cleaning a bedroom if she could see inside. It was lovely. The Early Natal décor was charming. When Kate gave a favourable report to the guys, we knew it was an extremely high standard! She is really fussy. We booked in for the night. The evening meal was superb, and with full tummies we walked back to the *rondarvels* (round thatched cottages) breathing in the crisp mountain air and enjoying the sounds of crickets, night *noo noos* (bugs) and the odd dog or jackal howling. We slept like logs.

The next morning, after a perfect breakfast which included the 'full English', followed by whole-wheat toast, muffins, scones and fruit, we set off to explore the *Midlands Meander*. This is a well organised enterprise of local people in this farming district who work from home. In a beautifully presented brochure with a map, there are lists of all the places you can visit. There are about fifty in all, including art galleries, woodcarvers, shoe makers, potters, toy makers, cheese and German sausage makers, restaurants and tea rooms. These provide excellent outlets for home crafts, and some businesses are even reaching factory-manufacturing size.

The Midlands Meander brochure also gives a brief description of each outlet or stop, some with photos too. It's just as well. Many of the farms are really huge, thousands of acres. From the main road to the house, one may have to navigate along a dirt track, or in one case, a dry river bed. (I wonder what happens in the rainy season!) We spent the day happily admiring weaving (bought table mats), a wood carvers studio (Allan bought a large bowl) and wonderful oil paintings of the majestic mountains that we longed to buy to take back to England (Kate bought a super one). Having done considerable damage to our wallets and credit cards, we returned to base.

It was such a lovely weekend that seemed to be much longer. Kate had to work the next week, so Bill, Granville and I took day trips, read, relaxed, walked around the area and, joy for Granville, we were only a fifteen minute walk away from Pick 'n Pay (a large supermarket chain). He stocked up Kate's kitchen (cooking is not her first love) and happily took over the cooking. Kate was delighted to relinquish her post!

"My fridge has never been so full, and I hate cooking for you because you are such a wonderful cook," she said with her typical candour.

I know how she feels. Granville is such a superb cook; it is not easy when you are cooking for an expert. Somehow one always feels inferior, and no matter how carefully you follow your favourite tried and tested recipe, it is not quite as good when you serve it to someone you know is great in the kitchen.

We spent a couple of days with Gregory, who had decided that he was not going to remain in South Africa. He felt that it would be better to continue his studies back in England. He had also been told that affirmative action was very much in evidence and, naturally, the preference for jobs went to blacks, asians or mixed-race applicants. When he told me this, I recalled what a young lad had told me on receiving a job offer.

"You know, Mama…I think I got this job because I am black. I want to get a job because I am the *best one*…not because I am black."

Several day trips were to our old home town. I had lived in the Hilton area from 1973 until we left for England. This beautiful green area cuts a swathe either side of the main road to Johannesburg, the N3, which starts just up the Fields Hill out of Pinetown, on through Kloof and Hillcrest and all the way up the hill to Shongweni and Assegai (approximately 15 kilometres). You can see that this is a wealthy area. There are golf courses, leisure centres, large country homes, shops and boutiques catering to the affluent shoppers. Further up, the freeway passes the farming districts of Cato Ridge, Camperdown and, after the turning off to Richmond, there is a long stretch until you reach Pietermaritzburg. Then a few miles up the hill is the little town of Hilton, which is just over 90 kilometres from the coast at Durban.

"Wow…this has changed. Big time!" said Allan.

We had a super morning tea with apple tart and lemon meringue pie and huge cups of tea. Then, after 'letting out some tea', we continued on our journey out to Sweetwaters. It was unavoidable— the road where Lucy had her accident. I glanced briefly at Allan as we drove past.

There was a fleeting look of pain; the same as I saw on his face when he watched her die.

7

Some Strange God

I wrote this story shortly after Lucy died in 1995. I called it 'Some Strange God'. It's a raw but honest account of my feelings and thoughts at the time.

ೲ

26th December 1995

Today is Boxing Day, 1995. Lucy-Jane died twenty one days ago, and now the house is quiet for the first time. Granville and the boys have gone to the beach—surf boards stacked inside the VW kombi.

So now I will write up my dairy. I usually write each day, but the pages are blank from the 4th December, as if my life stopped. More bouquets arrived earlier today. We now have forty-five, as many as my years. Monty, Lucy's little Yorkshire terrier, is sitting by the front door waiting.

She had many nicknames; she was the kind of special child that attracted them, but latterly, I called her Baby-Bat. I gave her that one when she turned eighteen and got her driver's licence. 'Bat' stood for 'Bat-out-of-Hell'. Traffic officers caught Lucy speeding two days after she got her driver's licence and said she was a Speed

Queen like her mother. The day after she died, they sent a large bunch of golden yellow roses: *For our lovely Lucy, From the traffic department, with love.*"

A few of the policemen came to her funeral, looking hot and uneasy in smart beige and blue uniforms. There were boys and girls with jaws tight, not wanting to cry. Her young friends were there too: now-solemn chaps she had danced with, and girls she had giggled with and brought home, calling out, "Hi, Mums, this is Amanda/Kate/Jake/Peter/Carl…or whoever."

Lucy was so beautiful inside, and she was lovely to look at. People were drawn to her. Wherever she went, heads turned around to look at her. The husband of my best friend, who knew her from a small child, commented that she was such an ugly duckling when she was growing up, but now she was 'drop dead' beautiful. Peculiar words now, I guess. Many times, men would stumble staring at her. I saw someone walk into a tree and, on another occasion, a traffic light. Strangers came up to her and would say, "You are so lovely."

She would react with exasperation, "Don't be mad; they are so silly, Mumsy. So silly."

She had clouds of long, golden, curly red hair, a perfect nose, even white teeth, fine smooth features and wonderful warm, caring eyes. Her hands were elegant, and she was five foot six inches tall and shapely—not too thin and not too fat. She had a proud deportment without snobbishness. She did not think she was anything special to look at, this gentle and humble soul, but she was exceptionally beautiful. She wasn't a pretty child and was an even uglier baby.

Born six weeks prematurely, she was pink and translucent with veins throbbing just below the surface of the dry, fluffy skin. Lucy was my firstborn. Late one night when my waters broke, the doctor said, "Pop into the hospital, and I will see you later. We must try to delay labour because your baby is too small." Later, he called in to see me at the hospital.

"How are you, my girl?"

"I think the baby's coming out," I replied.

"Let's have a look."

He saw a little head when he lifted the blankets. "Oh my God, she's crowning!"

Lucy-Jane was born quietly to an unprepared young mother just before the sun rose at St. Mary's Mission hospital, Kwa Zulu Natal. At first, she could not cry—just made squeaky noises. When she no longer needed the incubator, I took her home.

What do I do with this squirmy girl-baby?

She was this totally encapsulating dimension of little human-animal needs: feeding (bottles, warmers and sterilises), washing (forever washing clothes and baby) and emotional caring. It was all alien to me.

I was active in business and was used to working a twelve- to fourteen-hour day, but this was different—far more demanding mentally, emotionally and physically. I was so tired…drained; every part of me given out. There were times of rocking, holding and singing Zulu, English and Afrikaans lullabies in the rocking chair made of African Tambuti wood.

"Tula, tula, lala lala…[Quiet, quiet, sleep sleep]."

We would often both fall asleep in the chair until the next feed. Slowly, the tiny creature turned into a baby—not to get prettier then, but to change from infant to baby to toddler to child—a child with a round face, a dear little redhead with very little hair for at least two years. When the baby teeth came, there was a big space between the two front ones. She wasn't a pretty child, but she was so happy. She had a mature tenderness like a concerned house-guest.

Sorry to trouble you. Would it be all right if I had a feed now? Hate to put you to any bother but please can you change me, I'm really smelly.

I used to put her down for the night's sleep and could see she wasn't sleepy. I was, by eleven or twelve at night. Often when I woke (to have a wee), she would still be awake in the early hours, content to play in her cot and softly talk or tunelessly hum to herself. My little insomniac would watch me (on the loo) through the bars of her cot with knowing eyes, always patient and happy to see me. Did she know she needed to cherish every moment? That her days were on short time? It was curious that she did not like to sleep.

As long as she could see or hear me, she was happy. She preferred to be touching me. If I was sewing or baking or working in the garden, she would sit close, leaning like a warm sticky puppy against me. It drove me demented. Sometimes I wanted to be alone.

"Go away…Mummy wants to be alone." But she could not understand. She would sit outside the shut door, waiting. "Lucy, go away. Just go away," I would shout. Much later when I opened the door, she was sitting there with her upturned, guileless face and a big smile. "Sorry, baby, sorry! I needed some space, but you don't understand, do you?"

Years later, I met an acquaintance who had heard that I was divorced. "Ag, ja…ek het jou met 'n meisie gesien." [I saw you with a girl]. She was inferring that I had a gay lover.

Lucy was always so affectionate. She often held my hand and walked with me or gave me lots of hugs and kisses. Obviously, this was misconstrued.

"Listen, Baby-Bat, please stop kissing and cuddling me in shopping centres. People think I am gay."

Lucy was totally unconcerned and giggled, "Who cares, Mums? I love you, funny bunny."

Those shopping trips were our escape from the boys and the business. We could spend hours trying on clothes, perfume and shoes before returning home footsore but having had totally relaxed, happy times. We would talk for hours over cups of coffee and fresh fruit salad from The Centre Court restaurant or eat carrot cake from

Juicy Lucy, the health-food restaurant. It was amazing how she could eat such volume and not gain weight.

She kept up a running commentary as we walked, sat in restaurants and coffee bars or drove around. She was so funny. We just looked at one another and knew what the other was transmitting. Sometimes we laughed 'til we ached.

"Hey, Mums! That pervert is staring at me."

"Don't be vile, Lucy. He was just looking at you because you are so gorgeous." She would get mad when I said things like that.

"Don't be insane, Mums. I think they need glasses."

I remember once when we were at the Wild Coast Casino, a chap (total stranger) went down on his knees and said, "Angel-child, marry me, please."

"Dream on, sunshine! No! I don't need a husband," she said, walking away. Then, turning back with a big smile…"Hang on, are you rich?"

At 9.40 p.m. on the 4th December, the traffic police from the village phoned. I heard the ring like it was miles away. It sounded different: sad, serious and heavy. I was in bed, tired, exhausted but unable to sleep. Granville took the call. I knew it was bad news about Lucy, not one of the boys. I had often said to God, "Don't let anything ever happen to Lucy. *Not* my girl-baby, please. I couldn't live without her." Somehow, I knew that it was one prayer God would not answer.

They would not let me near the twisted car. The lights were spinning, noisy, harsh blue and silver—rescue lights. The police said to Granville, "Tie her down, keep her back…do anything, but do not let her near the car."

We told Gregory and Patrick what had happened then we went to get Allan from his cottage in the country. "Your sister has had an accident."

His 'dozy' face creased, puzzled…"What…what…what happened, Mom?"

We phoned my Mom and Dad, Kate and Bill. Kate asked, "Is it bad? We're coming now. Find out what hospital they are taking her to?"

We told Gregory to wait at the house and let our house-guests in when they came home later. "I think it will be a long night, Love."

We went back to the surreal place and waited with the lights flashing in our faces. It happened on 'Devills Corner', half a mile from our home in Hilton. Earlier that evening, Lucy and Allan had enjoyed a meal together at the hotel where she worked part-time. Allan said she was happy, chatty and full of nonsense—just being Lucy.

For more than an hour, the paramedics worked to untangle her from the car. I will never forget the squeal of metal-cutting equipment, spooky cable-floodlights and the throbbing generator.

"Please let me see her. She needs me. I just want to touch her, to let her know I am near," I begged. Then we followed the screaming ambulance down into Pietermaritzburg. Questions were spinning around in my head: *What on earth happened? Why won't they let me see Lucy? Is she in pain? What injuries has she got? Is her pretty face messed up? Will she be disfigured or crippled? Was she pushed off the road deliberately in an attempted hi-jack?*

On the day of the accident, I had an upsetting experience that was outside of my normal behaviour. I had a terrifying feeling of being trapped then tumbling and falling, of being out of control. These sensations were so intense and frightening that my friend, Esther, came to be with me. She called Granville and I together in the dining room, which smelled of old oak, brandy and Lemon Verbena potpourri. Holding our hands in hers, she said, "Stay together! You must stay together! Your two are going to walk through fire, so you must be close; close to yourselves and to God."

Hundreds of people from all walks of life came to her funeral: from alcoholic bar-flies to prissy church-goers; our Zulu nanny who had seen her grow from a toddler and called her Jabula (Happiness); Lucy's jazzy contemporaries, who were drawn to her effervescence; older people who loved the attention and loveliness; cousins, grannies and grandpas, aunts and uncles; father and stepfather, her brother and stepbrothers; and me. I was there, smiling, cushioned in a protective bubble, detached from the reality of the proceedings. His voice seemed to come from miles away, "Mom, she's dying, isn't she?"

"Yes, Allan, she's dying."

He was holding her hand under the bedclothes. Patrick was crying and stroking her arm. Gregory, standing a few feet from the bed with arms folded across his chest, standing straight and tall, kept muttering, "Oh no! Oh no! This can't be happening."

Patrick said, "Anne, Lucy is so cold. Shall I ask the nurse to bring her more blankets?"

The boys adored her, and she would cover for them when they came in reeking of drink at that silly time of madness that boys go through in adolescence.

"Mums, go away! He's not drunk, he's tired. Let him just sleep on my floor."

She would nurse them when they were hurting with girlfriend problems. They would be whisked off down to the Durban Beach to recover, surfboards strapped to her City Golf roof rack, windows open, loud music on the car radio.

"Young boys have delicate egos and such soft hearts. He's suffering, Mumsy," she would tell me off when I got cross with them.

We were so close for a mother and daughter. Too close. This is the extra pain thing. She virtually knew my thoughts and I hers. I don't ever want to have that oneness with anyone again because the pain of the parting is a gnawing hungry animal. This daughter told me lots I did not want to hear: she was no prude. I heard (in much detail) about the parties, college dances and dates…experiences she wanted me to share.

"No, Lucy, please no detail. I don't want to hear this stuff. Please, baby."

"But you have *got* to hear this, Mums. This is so exciting."

There was always something happening—busy and bright times, gatherings, parties and action, noise and long discussions with friends who had totally diverse upbringings, and young people in the house at all hours. Late into the night, they would be sitting on and around the kitchen table or sprawled in the sitting room or on the deck overlooking the pool. I would pad through sleepily for a glass of water or tea.

"Excuse me, you're in my fridge! Do I know you?"

"Hi…I'm Andrew, Lucy's friend."

Then there was her first love, Tommy. He was absorbed into her family and friends. He was patient and kind and gorgeous. She loved him totally. He said of her to his mum, "I'll wait for Lucy. Once day I'm going to marry her".

They went out for just over a year, and then he was killed in an accident on the very same road, the same place (Devil's Bend) where Lucy's car crashed. It was almost three years to the day that she had her accident. How bizarre!

This is how she wrote of Tommy's death in her dairy. I read it in the still hours of yesterday morning.

January 2nd 1995

I woke with a start, which I do now and probably will for the rest of my life. Sitting next to me so close was my mother. She was crying. Tommy's mom on the phone…Tommy had an accident…Tommy is dead.

I felt violently sick. My world crumbled, spun

around me. I wept. Thinking was painful, speech was impossible. My life as I knew it was over. I still ask myself, 'Why me?'

I could not move. I shook uncontrollably. Was I dreaming? This couldn't really be real. Please God, no.

I was treated like a sick animal. People tip-toed around me. Nobody mentioned Tommy. I hated that above everything. I clung to anything I could of his. I smelt him, I saw him in my dreams, he was never out of my mind. He was my life. I saw his mom, dad and sister. It was so hard. I sat in his room, surrounded by him, his clothes, pictures, letters…some to me, from me. I touched everything. I didn't want him to leave me. I am all alone. Next to his bed was his St Christopher. He hadn't worn it. He was not a Catholic, but he felt safe with it on. His Dad gave me his ring that he was wearing. It was still covered with his blood.

I love him. I loved him like nothing I ever loved before. Will I ever love that way again?

People sent me cards, flowers, people visited. Who were they? I cried all day most days and nights. Everything reminded me of Tommy. The funeral was my first. He was there in body; his soul is in heaven. I hated the Pastor. He didn't know Tommy. I did. It was over. Mom took me to Tommy's house. It was filled with strange people. No one knew what I was going through. My boyfriend, my lover, my life—he is dead. The man I planned to share the rest of my life with was gone. My life must be over. My mom was there…always. She loves me like no one else I know. I love her for that. She is always there for me. I hated people for not understanding. I wanted the whole world to know how much I love him, how much he means to me. What a wonderful, beautiful, loving, caring person he was. All I wanted was to talk about Tommy.

After Tommy died, she cried for weeks, slept in our bed, and I woke often to her sobbing. Although she rose above the pain, it was there just below the surface. I saw it often. Lucy had an entourage of so many different types of friends. Some were quiet and wimpy, some beautiful, rich, spoilt and 'glitzy'. She loved people no matter how strange they were. They delighted in the attention she gave to them.

When she was studying at college, she worked part-time at the local hotel bar. I once asked her if she knew how to mix drinks.

"Of course not!" she replied, looking at me as if I had mentioned something obscene.

"I just let them mix their own (drinks). Opening the cans and bottles would wreck my nails."

There she was *paid* to listen to all kinds of people's lives, and she loved them, enjoyed their stories and accepted almost everyone. If she *really* didn't like someone, she would smile in a quiet, condescending, secret way, and I knew she was just being nice.

After work or a date, no matter how late she returned home, I would feel her little Yorkshire terrier at the foot of my bed spring to action. Monty heard her car coming down the drive. Shortly afterwards she would run in, followed by the dog, and leap on the bed bursting with excitement. There was always a new story, descriptions of people she had seen, or sometimes a new local *skandaal* (scandal). Monty, happy to see her, lay on his back as she raked her long fingernails through his tummy hair.

"Guess what? Mumsy, this is soooo hysterical! Wake up!

Hey…you're not listening," she would say, her face close so that I could smell and feel her breath. I had glimpses of many lives, excitingly embellished. She had many friends from all walks of life and social strata. There were people who loved her and who followed her everywhere. There were sad, lonely, and peculiar people she took pity on and gave them her attention too. Even the funny looking guys—she was so sweet to them.

"Ag, shame, he's so ugly only his mommy could love him!"

She was three years old when Allan was born. She watched the newcomer for a few days with hesitancy, then she started to love him. Once, she saved his life. That is another story.

I met a young chap last Saturday that I had not seen for years. His family were our neighbours when the children were growing up. He was a nice boy, although quite snotty from his private schooling. He asked after Lucy and Allan and was devastated to hear Lucy was dead. His face crumbled.

"Oh, no, she was beautiful. And you know Auntie Anne, I have never known a brother and sister so close and so happy together."

A few years after my first marriage ended, I remarried. Lucy was twelve. She withdrew for a while. At first she greeted Granville and her stepbrothers with caution, then she pulled them into her sphere, and they loved her too.

Five hours after the accident, they finally let me near Lucy. The life support machines were bleeping—curved lines of light prolonging her life, the rhythm of air whistling in and out.

When she was born and first put into my arms, I unwound the tight hospital binding, studying her little body. She had tiny toes, huge long feet, and peeling skin, long lovely hands and fine delicate fingers, a scrawny body, but all the parts were there.

"Hello, funny little pink thing—this is the mummy part of you!"

Twenty-one years later, I lift the bedclothes. Her body from the shoulders down is still perfect—not even a broken fingernail (her pride). Smooth, silky, soft tan skin with pale brown freckles, boobs to side, hip bones, neat-twist tummy-button, downy ginger pubic hair, long legs and manicured toenails on lovely feet. Her head was at an uncomfortable angle, her long curly hair matted with blood. I want to rearrange the pillows and wash her hair—she hated dirty hair.

"Her hair is dirty. Is she in pain?" I ask the critical-care nurse.

"No, Mrs Shannon, she can't feel a thing. She is deeply unconscious'.

I touch her face, stroke her hair and tell her, "Baby Bat, you have been in a terrible accident. Your head is bashed in at the back, but you are still beautiful. Baby, I love you so much I want to stay here all the time, but the doctors want to help you and say you must rest. Sleep gently. I'm going home now, but I'll see you in the morning." Tears came into her eyes, and she moved a little. I wanted to stay and keep talking her through the weird production.

"Please go home and get some rest, and let your daughter rest," the neurosurgeon said firmly. It was typical doctor preparation, which, interpreted, meant: "God knows that sooner or later I have to tell them there is no hope, but let these poor things have a night's rest."

My sister, her husband, Ryan (eldest nephew), Allan, Patrick, Gregory, Granville and I were all at that hospital. It was after three in the morning when a doctor said 'time would tell'. We went back home. I lay down but didn't sleep.

At shortly after six that morning, as I was driving down from Hilton to the hospital, I was planning.

She is going to take ages to recover. Thank God we have an easy house, all on one level, and the wooden deck is a great place to sit and recover.

Will she need a wheelchair or crutches? It could be a long recovery. Hope she will be able to dance and run again, laugh, be silly, ride her horse…one day get married and have babies. Hope the injuries will not change her life.

I phone our Zulu house-maid from my cell phone. She gets in about 7.00 a.m.

"Regina, something terrible has happened to Lucy," I explain to her in simple English. I know she will be crying and praying as she works around the house. She is a devout, believing Christian who had been a special part of our lives for years. I know she will tell the African network—more effective than any news media—and I know our pain will be her pain as it has been many times in the past.

We arrive at Grey's Hospital, and the machines are still wheezing and bleeping. Lucy is alabaster, lying very still, her hair tumbling in curls all over the pillow. There always seems to be acres of it. Someone has washed it and put a little white bow in it, pulling it to one side. I took the bow out. She hated frilly things—ribbons and bows.

My beautiful Lucy. When, at what point, did she get to be pretty? When did the ugly duckling change? I did not notice the metamorphosis. It must have been gradual, but one day I noticed that she was much taller than me.

Her hair attracted attention first—masses of curly hair an incredible colour, golden red, soft as wool and so fine, tied up in bunches or loose. Writing now, I shut my eyes, and I can see her. Smooth, slightly freckled skin, soft little nose, full (really full) mouth and even white teeth. Long limbs, long fingernails perfect little boobs. Firm long neck—tight small curls at the back hairline. It is so strange. I can remember each part of her. The deep scar from a boil, chicken pox and the broken collarbone where her horse threw her in the veldt. Naked or dressed, sloppy in track suit or jeans or stunning in evening dress, her full lips with loads of natural gloss lipstick and clouds of perfume surrounding her. I see her at all stages, in a tableau of changing circumstances: happy face, sad face, funny face, quiet face, noisy, naughty, cheeky and concentrating, determined …stubborn. All those attitudes had so short a time-span.

"How is she today?" I ask.

The nurses are not looking into my face. They are busy scuttling around the ward. The neurosurgeon called me up to his rooms.

"Your daughter has brain-stem injury. I am *so* sorry. At best she will be blind, paralysed and unaware of her surroundings (in other words in a vegetative state). I can operate, but there really isn't much hope. What do you want me to do?"

I try to take it in.

"Operate, what for? To prolong the pain?"

"True," he says, quietly looking straight at me.

"No, just leave her," I said walking out.

I want to say (but I don't), *Look Doctor, Lucy believes in Jesus. She believes in another life, in another place where there is no sadness, no fear, no pain. I will have the sorrow, but she will be fine, so we can let her go. Don't worry.*

I do *not* say this because I think he will think I'm a religious nut.

Then we stayed with her—holding her, stroking her, talking to her and praying with her. There was a steady stream of family and friends in and out of the intensive care ward.

"Mom, you know, Lucy did tons of stuff for me," Allan said.

I thought back to when they were little kids. Lucy fussed around him continually—a devoted companion. We were really worried because they had their own language and sometimes we could not understand him. She interpreted for us, sometimes in an exasperated voice, "Mums…he wants to go for a *walk*; Mums *that* means he has done pooh."

When he was two, we took him to a child specialist, thinking he had a serious a physical problem which prevented him from talking. The only word that we could understand until he was nearly three years old was, *voetsak* (Afrikaans word meaning 'scat – go away').

He would yell at the wild dogs that came into our kitchen to steal our cats' food.

When he started to talk, it was fluent, as if he had been thinking the words all along but couldn't be bothered to verbalise. He was content to communicate with Lucy in their secret language.

I looked up to see a shabby old man standing a few feet from the bed. He was crying, sobbing. He said Lucy had made his life worth living. "She can't die. She is too lovely to die," he said over and over. He was one of the regular drinkers at the hotel where she'd worked.

Throughout that day, our extended family and also many of Lucy's young friends came to stand quietly by her bed, their faces blotchy from crying. Some were distraught, frightened in the alien world. It made me feel so grateful that they cared enough to visit that place.

"Thank you, you are so kind to come," I said.

Dying, she still looked lovely, so it was not a horror spectacle for them. I know they will miss her. I know that they will never forget being here. I knew her longer, and she knew me better than anyone. She was my very best friend. Lucy drew in the sunshine and, as the mother of a beautiful child, I basked in the glow.

"Is that your daughter? My God…she's divine," someone said.

But the most amazing secret joy was the closeness I had always shared with her, and in those minutes alone with her, I told her how much I loved her. I know she already knew, but I still kept telling her.

"Love you, beautiful baby."

"Lucy, you are such a brat to leave me. I know you have peace. You will be with Jesus, and I will see you again."

And I told her too, "Lucy, you are so loved. People from all over are sending their love."

There must always be the temptation to glorify the dead. Could it be that you forget the faults, remember only the good things, good habits, good times? I sift my memory for anything I did *not* like about her when such thoughts came to me the during past weeks, but I couldn't find anything horrible. She was gentle, sweet and beautiful. People loved her.

When none else was around I prayed quietly, stroking her hair, "Thank You, God, for Lucy. Thank You for giving me this truly wonderful child. Thank You, Jesus, for peace."

At some stage, a pretty little nurse sat with me when I was talking and praying, and she said, "You have some strange God. This intensive care ward is full of old people. Why didn't He take one of them. Why this beautiful girl? God, why her?"

"Sorry, I don't have an answer. He *is* some strange God, but he *is* God."

All day people came in and went out. A busy muddled day. Someone is always with Lucy, holding her, touching her, stroking her, talking to her. Allan brought a silver ring and put it on her finger. Her closest girlfriend put some Red Door perfume on her and flowers started arriving.

You darling people! But I don't think she can see you.

In the evening, as I held her, I felt that she was being tugged in another direction. She was pulling slowly away from me...I couldn't cry. The machines were flashing and making horrible sounds. There were clattering hospital noises, voices and medicinal smells. Shortly before the machines stopped there was a different smell—sad, sharp, and distinctive. I can't forget that smell. Just after sundown, she died.

We surrounded her, touching and holding some part of her. Her skin changed to glassy-white, and her eyes were suddenly empty. She wasn't there anymore. I buried my face in her neck, breathing her in for the last time. "Lucy, my Lucy, I love you."

"Okay...let's go," I said. We slowly walked out. Patrick didn't want to leave, and I pulled him away. "Come on Patrick...come now. She's gone."

Allan was standing by the door, staring back at his sister. The intensity of the pain in his eyes was terrible. I prayed that I never, ever see that look again.

ひひ

Today I read over my diary, recording those events, confining them to a few pages, trapping them in time. I am glad I wrote it down. My feelings were raw, and I remember thinking, *One day the pain will go away.*

But it hasn't.

8

Living and Breathing Africa

How do I feel seven years later? How do Allan, Granville and her stepbrothers feel? We keep our thoughts and only share them on rare occasions. Allan had not been back to Africa since we left in 1996. Sometimes I can see that the wounds are evident but not raw. For me, the scar tissue grew over the injury, and I got used to the loss. This pain belongs to me, and I guard it like a dog with a bone—a bone that he doesn't want but doesn't want to part with either. I feel that no one else deserves my pain or the powerful memories, so I seldom discuss them except with close friends and family. Allan and I talk about Lucy, and sometimes we laugh until we cry. There is so much to remember. She was so funny; she was so precious.

There are times when I can see her clearly in my mind, hear her voice, smell her perfume, and feel that she is very close. I miss her so much more with each year that goes by. The knife turns every time I see her friends getting married, having babies, or sometimes if I see someone who looks like her, and for one millisecond I think, *There she is! She's not dead. It was all a sick dream!*

Not long ago in Esher, near to our home in England, I followed a girl with a mop of golden curls—she looked so much like Lucy. But why? I know she's dead. A very small part of me believes she isn't—that this is a nightmare, and I will wake soon.

A really weird thing happened the Sunday before she died. Granville and I attended an evangelical church in Hilton. Usually, just the two of us went to the Sunday morning service. As they got older, past the Sunday school stage, we didn't force our kids to go to church, but we always asked, "Who wants to go to church?"

On Sunday, 3rd December, Lucy said, "Yes, wait for me Granni (her pet name for Granville). My life is such a mess. I want to come to church with you guys."

During the service, the speaker (visiting from England) stopped midstream. He was preaching about forgiveness. He looked over the congregation and said, "I need to speak to someone here today. I have an urgent message from the Lord."

Oh, yea…one of those hysterical preachers! How awful. I hate emotion and drama.

Then he got down from the platform and walked straight up to where we were sitting, right at the back of the church. There must have been about 400 people in the congregation, but he seemed to focus only on Lucy. Then he leaned over a row of people to put his hand on her shoulder.

"What's your name?" he asked.

"Lucy," she said, going bright red, gripping my hand and looking at him with widened eyes.

"Lucy, there have been painful times in your life, and many people have hurt you. In Jesus' name, you must forgive them. I want everyone here to know that many people will come to know Jesus because of you. As Jesus forgives you, you must forgive too." With that, he turned and walked back towards the platform, leaving us still holding hands, too shocked to be embarrassed.

That preacher could never have known what turmoil she had been through in her twenty-one years: learning difficulties at school, thorny times with her father, our divorce, serious illness, the death of her first love three years ago, and, since his death, a succession of young men who let her down. She was so naïve…she let it happen again and again. She trusted too much.

As we drove back home from church that early December day, Lucy said that she had given her life to Jesus. She would obey him, and she wanted to walk in His way. She had forgiven and was forgiven. She said she felt calmness and peace as never before. The next day, she had her accident. The following day, she died. These incredible supernatural happenings re-enforced my belief in Jesus Christ as Lord and Saviour and that no matter how terrible, these events were a part of God's plan for my life, and Lucy's!

How strange that my faith should be strengthened by that terrible loss. I accepted Jesus as my Lord and Saviour when I was a little girl. I remember the day, the time, and the place. I was brought up in a loving Christian home, but I still felt that I needed to let Jesus into my heart, which I did on 5th August 1956, when my father explained Acts 16 verse 31 to me. (Believe on the Lord Jesus Christ and you will be saved). I was only a child, but I had a simple belief and trusted that God was listening to my prayer. I remember an amazing feeling of peace, and I knew God my father had done something that would always keep me safe.

Years later when I went to art school, my faith was tested, and I searched and studied other avenues and religions in a serious, intellectual way.

"You have been brainwashed!" my 'flower-power' buddies told me, but no one had anything better nor could offer me the peace, sense of order and the logic of God's plan for me and for mankind. I saw it at work in my family, in my Christian friends and in the reality of the presence of God in my life. Jesus was and is a living reality. One thing, one very important lesson I have learned is that Christians are people—people with Jesus Christ in their lives, but still with much of themselves and their foibles remaining.

"I *am* a Christian but just human, trying to live life honestly," I have told people when they ask about my belief in Christ. "I try to please my Lord, try to live sincerely and truthfully in the context of today and my life. I may mess up (probably will), and I may let you down, but Jesus will *never* let you down. The nature of God is revealed in Jesus Christ his Son. He is pure truth and only good, and only good is *not* what I am."

After Lucy died, there were many friends and wonderful people who gathered around to help me through that horrible time. I found that I was in a translucent bubble that protected me from the stark reality that my daughter was dead. There were bunches, vases and pots full of flowers. The following week, the local florists started to delay the deliveries so that instead of eighteen arriving in one day, they staggered the deliveries, and we received at least two a day from each of the florists. I can't remember how long it went on for, but we had bouquets every day for weeks and weeks.

There was a double whammy that added to the sadness for our family. Our gardener and general handyman, Philemon, who had lived in a kia (cottage) on the far boundary of the garden for seven years, went missing. He was due to return on Sunday after visiting his family that weekend. The same Monday of Lucy's accident, we were wondering where he was because he hadn't returned home after a weekend away. Regina and several black friends asked where Philemon was…we just didn't know. He was honest and very reliable. It was most unusual.

As the week passed, we became totally enveloped in the activity surrounding Lucy's death. Then, on the weekend, his children came from the township to search for him. Granville assisted by phoning hospitals and local police stations.

"Yes," said the Albert Falls police, "We have the body of an unidentified male who was involved in a hit and run accident on Sunday evening."

Granville went to the state mortuary. It was Philemon. My black friends came to mourn Lucy and Philemon's death. (And wow! They know how to do it properly!) It is part of their tradition to weep, wail and howl. Instead of flowers and cards, their love was demonstrated in physical crying, sitting at the gate of the house and with bowed heads, extending an upturned hand supported by their other hand, swaying slowly from side to side. One old tribal leader came with his daughters to *share my tea* (spend time with me).

He said, "We can't give you back your daughter, but we show you our sorrow. We come to cry for Lucy, and we come to help you to give her back to the family that you cannot see [her ancestors]."

The Zulus believe death is just a return to the ancestral spirits, and the only loss is to those remaining behind. It's not too far apart from what we as Christians believe. Maybe that is why they so easily accept the love of God the Father, the sacrifice of Jesus, the power of His Holy Spirit and the hope of the resurrection to a new body and eternal life.

I told him that we were not sure if Lucy had been pushed off the road, whether she was responsible for the accident, or what in fact had happened. (There was a rumour that someone saw a Toyota Hi-Ace taxi swerve and speed off at about the same time and in the vicinity of the accident). My wise old African friend said, "Mrs Annie, if Miss Lucy was pushed (off the road), it was by someone with too much sorrow, too much hate. Don't let your anger burn your heart. It will hurt you and your family too much."

Weeks later, when I told him that I may have been going overseas, he said, "This is good. Africa belongs to us...the black people. After a storm, the rivers are always dirty and full of trouble, and it will be time before the waters of run clear. It is good to go, but you will come back."

He knew that I had stood with his people to give them back the rightful authority of which they'd been robbed. He knew I hated the system that had imprisoned the blacks mentally and physically, that had kept them servants of the white *baas* [boss] and *medem* [madam].

I thought back to the terrible apartheid years when the white regime in power tried desperately to break the spirit of the black people. I know I have no right to feel angry towards the newly released black nations.

Yes, it was their time. It was time for Africa to be run by the indigenous nations. These wonderful resilient, patient people understood what was needed to unite the geographical areas that had been isolated into the separate countries by the 'homelands' policy created Dr Verwoerd (the architect of Apartheid). They also knew that there had to be a change in the hearts and attitudes of all people to create a spirit of reconciliation and forgiveness..

I hope they will be fair and just during the coming years of change, and that they will forgive the things that bad white people with power did to them. I am so happy that they have strong minds. Apartheid did not break their spirit. Adversity often strengthens. I love that strength and resilience, the power of forgiveness, love and freedom that millions of previously suppressed people are showing in this emerging rainbow nation.

ဿ

Allan, Granville and I walked, drove and wandered from place to place in and around our old neighbourhood in Kwa Zulu Natal. Our house, in the smart part of town, looked sad…the Jacaranda trees seemed older and stronger, but the town was vibrant with new life.

As the shackles of apartheid have fallen off, more black people can afford cars, and the town is bustling with smartly dressed young people of all race groups.

At local feed and livery suppliers, the 'Old Natal' set in tweed and twin-sets mingled and merged with the modern 'mink and mature' generation, casually dressed in riding clothes, jodhpurs and riding boots, their four-by-fours parked outside (muddied, but reeking of wealth). The property business was booming, and I couldn't resist looking in estate agents' windows. I worked as an agent in *this* country area until I left for England.

"Wow, these prices are insane," I told Granville. "They have doubled since we left."

Allan has bought more curios—a massive Zulu blanket and two wooden giraffes that each stood three feet high.

"How on earth are you going to get them back to England on the plane?" I asked.

"You can't have that lot stuffed in the overhead lockers. Those giraffes will impale someone if they fall out!" Kate added.

While I am looking at some carved bowls I hear, "Hey, Annie, where have you been?"

I turn to see one of my old clients from the area—William Glendenning. I had done several transactions for him, the first many years ago. I sold him his first piece of land when he was a single chap. His shy, gentle wife, Jan, was beaming behind him. "Hi, Anne, How wonderful to see you!"

They told me that they had both given up their careers as solicitors to buy a curio shop in the tourist area. They were doing really well in business but were worried about future opportunities for their children. They felt that the government's policy of affirmative action would create a situation whereby their boys (now in high school) would find it difficult to find jobs after having leaving school. They asked us about life in England. They were thinking of emigrating to either England or Australia.

We saw several people we knew that day. Some had changed very little, and others looked older and tired. When we were in the bank, changing our pounds to rand, I saw Riana, a friend who was in school with me (actually we were in the same class all through primary school). She looked wonderful. After hugs and 'how are you', I said, "Seriously, Riana, you look fantastic. You must have lost about twenty kilograms, and your skin is glowing. Then I added quietly, "Hey, Riana, have you got a lover?'"

By the panicky look on her face, I think I may have guessed right! "Is it *that* obvious?" she whispered.

I am not sure how *I* looked to my friends and family who had not seen me for a few years, but I felt that I was a *totally* different person to the forty-five-year-old woman who left the neighbourhood seven years before. It was as if I had been on a long, tiring journey. It was great to relax and meet friends again, especially old friends.

We stopped for lunch at a restaurant overlooking the Valley of One Thousand Hills. This beautiful view, visited by many tourists from all over the world, typifies the Africa we cherished. We sat on the *stoep* (veranda) looking over the hills as they softened into the horizon. The valley lay below like a huge basin, filled and busy with the lives of thousands of families. They live mostly in traditional Zulu huts, but progress now offered the alternative brick or ash-block construction with a tin roof. Someone is banging. We search and find a chap sitting on top of a building, putting up the rafters. Myriads of mellow sounds travelled up to us together with the sound of children singing in harmonies only heard in Africa. As we waited for our food, the living show kept us occupied.

As the pretty waitress brought our food, I remembered that Lucy and I shared the same view in silence the day after her beloved Tommy was killed.

On that day in May as we ate, the spirit of Lucy is alive in that brave place. We all sensed her presence—more than we ever could in England.

The harshness of Africa brought back the soft places in our hearts. I know I shall be glad to be back in England's anonymity, but now, as I sat in the comfortable wicker chair and ate crispy bacon and avocado salad followed by cups of delicious tea, I kept glancing over the hills and breathing in the memories.

Kate had taken ten days leave from the practice where she worked in 'Maritzburg and had planned a holiday for us. She had booked us into a private guest house (Wyndford), in the Orange Free State. It was right on the Lesotho border.

We set off early one morning. Allan had moved down to the coast to stay with friends, so it was just us 'oldies'. Soon after Mooi River, we turned in towards the mountains—on the majestic Maloti Route. I had promised to visit Gemma, a young friend who worked as a tour guide and receptionist at the beautiful mountain resort called 'Little Switzerland'. The narrow road took us up a winding pass with breathtaking drops down hundreds of feet on either side. Granville opened the car window.

"Wow—we are so high up. The air even feels thinner…and look! That view is unbelievable! You can see *forever*."

"More like, you can see *eternity*," said Kate. "And hey, don't distract Bill. He needs to concentrate on driving or we'll all join the goats and rocks at the bottom of the valley!"

The hotel reception was busy when we arrived, but Kate and I first headed for the lavatories (many cups of tea needed to be released). Upon our return, we found Gemma: she was looking stunning.

"Hey, beautiful lady!"

She was delighted to see us, and there were squeals of joy.

"Mums—you found me!"

She has been Lucy's best friend, and we remained close friends after Lucy died. She also called me Mums. They'd met at the YWCA in Pietermaritzburg where Lucy had gone to study at the S.A. College of Health and Beauty. Gemma was doing her travel diploma at the technical college. They became great buddies.

Within six months, they were asked to leave the YWCA;

something to do with 'breaking every rule in the YWCA book'. Goodness knows what went on, but I heard some hair-raising tales of parties and lots of mad student fun.

Gemma has been through so much heartache in recent years; Lucy and another of her flatmates died within a short space of time, and now she was telling me of another tragic death.

"I am the only one left," she said dramatically. "Everyone's dying around me."

We started speaking about Lucy.

"I miss her so much, Mums, she was so incredible. I remember going to places with her. The guys use to drool over her, and she was so cool about it. She was just the best friend I ever had."

Gemma was called away by the manager, and we sat sipping our tea in the beautiful lounge. The surroundings were amazing. I walked to the window and gazed out at the beautiful mountains, craggy and strong, rising up directly behind the hotel. I started humming and just then Gemma came up behind me. I didn't hear her until she said,

"We used to *pay* Lucy to stop singing. She just couldn't keep a tune, and it drove us mad. Now I know her 'melodious' ability was handed down to her from her mother."

"Brat!" I said, smacking her bottom playfully. "Love you, Gemma," I said, hugging her, "but we need to reach our hotel by evening, so we must be going. We don't want to be lost in the bush. See you next time you're in England or we're back here."

We were heading for the Golden Gate National Park, which is on the Orange Free State/Kwa Zulu Natal border. The Golden Gate is a stunning rock formation that rises up either side of the road. There is a hutted camp with picnic site in the reserve, and this is where we are heading to stop to for the lunch that Granville had prepared early in the morning before we left. True to his exacting culinary standards, and even though it was a picnic, we had avocado pear with shrimps, stuffed eggs, an array of cold meats and fresh herb bread.

"No wonder you are fat, Annie," said Kate with her usual diplomacy.

What stunning scenery all the way through to the guest farm! The sky was intensely blue, the grass drying in various shades of gold. Mountains rose up like sharp blocks, and the hills almost obscured the farmhouses that lay tucked in their folds. Many of these homes dated back to before the Boer War.

I was relating to Granville, who had arrived in South Africa in 1980, that this area was the hotbed of Afrikaner power during the apartheid years. During that time, there were restrictions on black, coloured and Indian families: they could not travel freely in the area. In fact, no Indian could remain in the Orange Free State Province overnight! The blacks and coloureds, who were needed for domestic and farm work, were not subjected to the same demeaning law. The Indians, who were mainly traders in the area, had to leave the province at sundown. Granville couldn't believe it. He thought we were joking. He said he would 'check our facts' when he returned to civilisation.

We visited Clarens, a small arty town built around a monument square. The shops are mainly old houses converted into business premises with fantastically imaginative décor displaying excellent art from all over South Africa: local wines, handicrafts and the most wonderful country-style tea rooms which served homemade cakes *to die for*! Artists, local people and the 'rich and famous' (of South Africa, usually) meet in these shops and art galleries.

I was totally absorbed by one painting of the locale that made me reach for my credit card, but Granville came into the shop at that moment, and I was overcome with guilt seeing that I had just blazed him for buying a box of red wine. I wish I had bought it. The painting was of a winter hillside covered with shanty-shacks, little black children with ragged jerseys, no shoes on their feet, and old people wrapped in colourful blankets huddled in the doorways. The dry brown hills dotted with dark green trees reached far out to the vivid blue sky. It was gorgeous, and I can still see it in my mind's eye. There's a slice of life in that picture (I wonder who *did* buy it) that is pure Africa.

The dusty feet of the children, who now have the opportunity to be educated and get well paid jobs will one day be covered by really expensive leather shoes. It amazes me to see how much black people will spend on imported shoes. But they have been barefoot for too long.

Huge boulders and rocky hills surround Wyndford Country House Hotel—our home for the next week (or as it transpired, two). The homestead was built by Italian prisoners of war, and the setting is marvellous. We are just in time for afternoon tea under the large thatched cover in the pleasant, natural garden. The fresh chocolate cake and home-made rice biscuits are a foretaste of the superb food that the guesthouse offers. The whole atmosphere is 'old colonial', and after living in England for the past few years, I find it difficult to relax while the cheerful servants run around transporting things to the rooms, serving tea, and virtually carrying one along as well. We settle into our *rondavel* rooms with Biggy Best (South Africa's answer to Laura Ashley) décor and lie down on the beds for a late afternoon nap.

We surfaced an hour before dinner and were persuaded by the young guy who ran the guest-farm to take a walk along to the Lesotho border about a mile away. As he energetically set off along the rocky paths, I said to Kate,

"Hey! By the end of the holiday we will all be like *dassies* [rock rabbits]!"

I think he heard me because he slowed down. As we picked our way along a river-bed, Kate fell and cut her knee right down to the bone. Fortunately, we were only about 200 metres from the hotel, so she didn't have too far to walk. The next day, she showed us how badly she was injured. We think it should have stitches. She dismisses the suggestion, "Oh, stop fussing; I am not dying."

The next ten days were spent either in or around the guest farm, or we took short trips to small villages nearby. Kate's knee was really sore and had become infected, so we couldn't do too much walking (Thank God). Being out of the holiday season in South Africa, for several days we were the only guests. The atmosphere of the guest farm was so peaceful and calm, as if it had special air to relax the body and soul. The staff, mainly from Lesotho (just over the border), were charming. In the morning before breakfast (if we got up early enough), we heard them singing Christian hymns and choruses at the daily service held for the farm workers and hotel staff.

Kate and I had long discussions about all kinds of stuff that sisters and good friends talk about as we sat in the warm winter sun. We watched a malachite sunbird visiting the flowers nearby and the noisy weaver birds fighting about some housing dispute in their ranks. At mid-morning, the shy African maids would bring tea and cookies. The teapot, covered by a multi-coloured hand-knitted tea-cosy, provided us with several cups of tea before. Granville and Bill did some serious expeditions in the surrounding hills and would time their return perfectly. After tea, they would take off again on another walk or lie on the recliners reading out-of-date newspapers.

Some days, after morning tea, we drove to little villages, and twice we visited an angora bunny farm, run from an old farmhouse that is caught in a time warp. It was preserved and presented as if it was still the 1800s (right down to the lacy-cut newspapers on the shelves). The tropical garden, around which the farm-house and cottages were built, had old flat-crowned trees: Jacaranda, blue and white Agapanthus, and orange Clivea plants growing in the soft shade. It was constantly watered by hissing water sprayers. Tame guinea fowl, geese and chickens roamed around the garden and verandas of the house.

We could not resist buying gorgeous handcrafted angora knitwear from the home industry shop. Later, we walked around the farm and found a group of black ladies sitting in a circle, knitting the garments and articles for the shop. They were delighted to show us their work.

The quiet tin-roofed towns, space and the beauty all around us was soul food. I found myself relaxing on a completely different level from the usual annual holiday. Looking out of the car window one day, I thought how far removed it was from the frenetic business world I had left behind.

Completely and utterly different!

Each afternoon at the guest farm, we had a ritual. It started on the second day, and we kept it up until we left for home: We walked up the hill behind the farm to sit on large flat rocks. Gazing out over the valley and the Lesotho border post, there was a fresh tableau each afternoon. We watched, spellbound.

Boy chasing donkey jumps on its back then gets thrown off…boy chasing donkey; a man pulling a reluctant dog along by a rope around its neck, stopping often to shout at it (we think that maybe he is drunk); women carrying bundles of washing down to and from the river, or food home from the little trading store. We see queues of people wait patiently to get through the border gates. The children, either sauntering along or running back and forward like little ants, busy with the things that children do, many in their school uniform of white shirts and grey shorts or skirts, are always fascinating to observe. A total sense of contentment and peace absorbed us, and as the sun fell behind the mountain, the shadow very quickly moved over the valley and then over us, cooling us instantly. Slowly, we walked back to our rooms to wallow in deep, hot baths before making our way to the dining room to enjoy a fantastic dinner.

The original plan had been to travel on to the Eastern Transvaal after five days, but we just loved being there, so we extended our stay until Kate had to return to work. Unenthusiastically, we returned to Pietermaritzburg.

When I put my mobile phone back on, there were several messages from the office in England. I found myself feeling ratty that I even had to *think* about work again.

I have been keeping up my dairy, but I notice it no longer is separated into days. My life is no longer divided into half-hour appointments starting at 9.00 a.m. It is interesting that as I relax and savour the moments of my life, I feel that I am 'allowed' to write as little or as much as I want.

Granville set off for Pick 'n Pay early the next day, proudly carrying a large Lesotho basket. At the supermarket, he was in his element. When I saw him coming out of the shop, laden like a pack-horse, I reminded him that we had a long walk back with all the bags and packages, as well as his special basket (now stretched with its hoard). In his excitement, he had forgotten that we had to return home on foot. After moaning and groaning all the way back to Kate's kitchen, I clarified that his next trip would be solo.

The following Saturday evening, Kate and Bill treated us with a visit to a fish restaurant on Durban quayside. The diners sit just a few metres away from the huge ships and boats that pass into and out of the harbour. It's magical—lights reflecting in the slippery water, gulls squawking as they settle in for the night, bells ringing on the pier to announce each vessel that enters.

The food was superb, and we eat far too much. Kate's daughter, Helen, and her son-in-law joined us; it was lovely to be with them too. They are such down-to-earth sensible kids. Helen was born six weeks before Lucy. I have watched her grow from a cheeky little baby to a strong young woman with babies of her own.

Kate and I find ourselves remembering back to when we were children and how we had spent many Friday evenings on that same pier where the restaurant was now built. Dad was a keen fisherman, and I can still see him walking in the door of our house in Durban North straight from work. He smelled of industrial machinery grease and Brylcreme.

"Come on, Flo, you ready?"

Mom would have packed a basket with food and drink. Kate and I would be waiting in Dad's old Austin A40 long before take off. Our supper was usually curry and rice, which we ate out of Tupperware bowls. As it got dark, the huge rats and cockroaches would scuttle past, and once we rescued Dad's packet of bait just before it disappeared between a gap in the large concrete blocks that formed the pier. Mom, Kate and I would have some precious times together. She enjoyed being with us girls and would tell us jokes in a funny accent: some snippets of family history, gossip or incidents from her earlier days. To this day, I cannot decide whether or not they were true.

One that came to mind during this dinner was when her mum (Granny Samuels) was 'fed up to the back teeth' with grandpa because he was drinking too much. This particular evening, she was particularly miffed with the old boy: he'd been delivered in a paralytic state to the doorstep. She dragged him into the spare bedroom, undressed him and then proceeded to put clothes pegs all over his body, especially on the sensitive bits! As he came round (in great pain), he woke her and the girls with his screaming.

Helen said she thought it was just a family legend, but I don't think so. Granny Samuels was a very tough lady! She was a good mother who never let her girls down—full of fun, and she stood no nonsense. She was tall and dark, with beautiful, Jewish features that added strength to her face. Granny Samuels wasted no time on pity, nor did she allow her family to be anything other than 'get up and go' and 'don't let it get you down', no matter what the circumstances. She brought her four girls up during the Second World War, when times were hard, work was scarce and the men were away fighting in

Egypt. Even though South Africa was removed from a lot of the serious action, several thousand of the 'boys' joined the allied troops (especially the action in North Africa). Many never returned to the sunshine of Africa. South Africa was at war and was frequently used as a base where troops could recover and ships could dock for repairs. Many old soldiers or sailors fondly remember the hospitality and generosity they received from the people of Durban during the Second World War.

After the super fishy meal, we set off to drive back home. Within minutes, Granville was fast asleep, snoring loudly. Kate asked me if I was looking forward to going back to work. She said that she had noticed that for the past few days I had been a bit remote and absorbed. I tell her of my feelings.

"Kate, it's great to be a high achiever. There is joy in doing a job thoroughly, gaining favour with clients, having the satisfaction of completed projects and the progressive ambition to do even better. But as I switch-off from work, these feelings have become less important. I need to regain my life."

I continued explaining that I hoped it was not going to disappoint Granville and my boss too much, but I was probably going to resign. I just knew it was time to move on.

"Sometimes we have to stop…before we can grow," she said firmly.

The next few weeks, we spent in and around Durban and Pietermaritzburg, and we also visited my dearest friend Jenny and her husband Roderick, who live near Margate on the South Coast of Kwa Zulu Natal. I could write tomes about our friendship—she is intelligent, humorous, enterprising and an amazing example of a Christian who lives out a real and vibrant life. She runs several businesses and is involved in church work and outreach, especially to young black kids. She has great love for people in general. Although very busy with her various projects, she still prepared special meals for us and organised trips to local view sites.

On the day we were supposed to leave to return to Pietermaritzburg, Granville had an accident. As he was walking to the car, he cut his head badly on a T V mast in their back garden. Jenny's maid rushed to tell us that the *baas* was lying on the grass. We found him—knocked out cold—in a pool of blood. We took him to the local hospital, where he had several stitches to the cut.

The doctor suggested that we delay our trip until we were sure there was no further damage, so for the next few days, instead of going back to Kate and Bill, Granville lay on a recliner by the pool, reading books and writing. Jenny's two little dogs enjoyed his stable lap. He seemed to suffer no serious after-effects.

One Saturday morning, after we had returned back to Kate and Bill's home, we all went to a huge shopping complex—The Pavilion, near Durban. It had been one of my favourite shopping places with Lucy. We had spent many happy hours gossiping in the coffee bars, trying on clothes and shoes and doing girly things. I thought that it would be difficult to go back with all the memories lingering in that place, but actually, it was as if she was there and we still had to meet up. There was anticipation of something good about to happen.

In a rug and weaving shop where Allan was looking at a large colourful African wall hanging, I noticed a familiar face.

"What are you doing here, Caroline?"

I was then enveloped by a dear friend who I had known for forty-something years. From 1990 until we left to live in England, we ran our own estate agency business, and Caroline had joined us as a senior negotiator. It was super seeing her again, and we talked for ages.

"Don't you want a job? Don't you want to come back?" she asked suddenly.

"I am managing *Real Estates of Hilton*. Wow, I would so love you on board. We would just have to put an ad in the paper with 'Annie is back', and we would be inundated with replies!"

"What a mad idea!" I said, without thinking. Caroline and I arranged to meet up for lunch before we return to the UK.

"Think about what I said about the job," she added as we parted.

We continued shopping in the magic shops. Naturally, our British pound went a long way, and soon Granville and I were both laden with shopping bags. We stopped for a cappuccino at the Brazilian Coffee Bar.

I can smell Lucy's perfume and hear the clip-clop of her gold sandals on the tiles. I expect to have her join the table, but when I look around, she's not there.

Caroline's job offer occupied my thoughts. I knew that I could make a good living in the area—I knew it like the back of my hand! Did I really want to leave my well-paid position? Did I want to leave England? Why had we left South Africa in the first place? What had changed now to make me feel I could return? Had those problems gone away?

A week before we were due to return to England, Ryan asked us up to his farm for a *braai*. The drive through the Tala valley is spectacularly 'Africa'. There is a huge game reserve on the way, and it was special seeing wildebeest, giraffe, and several varieties of buck, as well as beautiful birds of all colours and sizes. The soil and grasses were dry, desperate for rain.

The far vistas in Kwa Zulu Natal are thrilling. It's wonderful to travel dusty roads for miles and miles and to see hills, valleys, bush and scrub-land in wide, wide open spaces. I love Africa. Somehow I think I will die here.

We reached the farmhouse gates. I had forgotten how high the fences were and how aware of safety each person travelling had to be. As he pacified the dogs and let us into the enclosure, we noticed that Ryan was fully armed. Why am I shocked?

Was it always like this? The guns, vicious guard dogs, burglar guards, the razor wire fences and gates?

153

"Hey broer [brother], check the *ammo* [guns]!" shouted Allan.

"*Ja*…part of the local uniform!" Ryan laughed.

Most of our immediate family were there—about fifteen in all. Helen had her little ones—the new baby (just a few months old) and Emma, who was three. Somehow, it hurt to see her with them. Lucy had been just six weeks younger than Helen, and Lucy had no babies. She would never have babies.

Emma took a shine to Granville. Little children often do. She asked him to read her a story. It was about a monkey with a long tail. Jokingly, Granville asked her, "Do you have a tail, Emma?"

"No," she said, shaking her head, "I've got no tail—but *daddy* has got a little one in the front."

We all laughed while Emma looked from one to the other with total innocence, wondering why we were all laughing.

That day, as I listened to the young people talk, make plans, laugh at the difficulties and shoulder the disasters, it gave me hope that the country had a future with these brave young people working towards a better life. This generation is strong and resilient. They love their country and are determined to work together, accommodating all the different people and race groups.

"It's all about tolerance and *wanting* to make it all work," said Elizabeth. "We're not leaving to go anywhere 'easier'; this is our country. It has its problems, but we can get through. I think the biggest problem is AIDS. It is wiping out hundreds of young people. They say that more than 40% of the work force is HIV positive. That's really shocking, but we just have to work at educating and getting the message across to the smple rural folk."

She told us an amusing story.

"The local health workers were doing a project in a remote area to try to encourage the rural people to use condoms. After lengthy explanations about the disease and how it is transmitted, the nurse demonstrated (using a broomstick) how the condom was to be fitted. Weeks later, the health workers revisited the area. Outside most of the huts in the village where they had given their talk and demonstration was a broomstick, and on the top, blowing in the breeze, was a condom!"

But then, neither the AIDS epidemic, *nor* the violence frighten these young people. Ryan's friend had been ambushed and shot dead in his *bakkie* [small truck] a few weeks earlier.

"Ryan, aren't you scared?"

"*Agh* no, Auntie Annie! If it's my time to pop my clock, I'll just have to go! *Yus*…you can't spend your life worrying about things."

After a beautiful day with our family, we returned as the sun was setting over the hills.

For the next few days, I couldn't get Caroline's job offer out of my mind…that and what would be involved in returning to South Africa.

We would have enough money to buy a small house. I know I would do well in the estate agency business again, but why did we leave originally leave? Was it the rising level of violence, the financial changes at the time, or was I really running away from memories of Lucy? In England, I can shut the door on the reminders and the pain of losing so many precious people from my life. Compared to England, the crime rate was incredibility high. In our old neighbourhood (private schools, large houses with tennis courts, pools and lovely green lawns), we found the razor wire topped fences was now as high as the fence boarders on the farms. Most men (and many women) carried firearms.

When I asked one of my friends from Hilton about the crime and violence, she said, "Shucks, it's much worse than when you were here. It's just not publicised."

I tried to 'think' us back into Africa. By that, I mean I tried to imagine what it would be like to live there again.

The good parts: sunshine, beaches, wonderful social life and friends, beautiful rugged countryside, better, bigger houses and servants to help keep the homes looking great. But then there are the guns, razor wire, guard dogs and serious security awareness. The violence was a major factor. I remembered back to when we were staying on the farm and Dad had a 'mayday' message from his neighbour. When he went to investigate, the farmer had been ambushed and shot with an automatic weapon at close range. He had no head. His young son of twenty was hysterical. That was only one incident of many that ran through my mind. But I guess there are several factors that attracted us to life in England. Although returning to South Africa could seem to be an option, I also feel that I would be running away from the pressure of the job in England more than wanting to move back to my home country. Examining my position in the company, the internal politics and the falling property market, I realize that there have been escalating stresses in my job (including having to retrench and pull back on staff privileges). Now that I am off my adrenaline high, I just knew I could not keep up the pace with someone else in control of my life. I have lost the will to motivate myself as well as the other staff—to carry on in a positive frame of mind. It's time to get off the hamster wheel that someone else is spinning for me!

During our year out of the business world, the restraints and tensions are falling off me slowly. As they drop, it is as if the liberty allows me to feel, to see and to experience things I have suppressed for so long: to admit to myself that it is time to move on in many areas of my life.

I met for lunch with my friend Caroline, who had offered me the job a few weeks previously. We had a super time reminiscing, and she gave me an update of the state of the market at that time. It was an extremely busy time for estate agents: the property business was booming. People were determined that they would enjoy their lifestyles in the context of the 'New South Africa'.

"South Africans with nowhere to run," Caroline said and added, "Now Anne, I was serious about the job offer. Just tell me when you are ready, and I will make sure there is a desk for you!"

"Caroline, I just don't know. I *never* say 'never', but I am really not sure. I love South Africa with a passion, but I have grown to love England too. I appreciate the changing seasons, the soft green countryside, and the magic of London with its art galleries, theatres and museums. When I am away from either country, there are things that I miss, but in England, it is easier *emotionally* for me. Here, especially in Hilton, I am reminded of Lucy around every corner. For now, my answer must be 'no'…but let's not close the door. Okay?"

"Of course," she said graciously.

Granville and I were walking to the supermarket early one morning. He carried his 'special' shopping bag and said as we left the house, "This time we are only buying bread and milk. We don't need anything else." I only *just* managed to stifle a laugh.

The path took us through some *veldt*, and we watched as a huge flock of *Hadedahs* jostled in a thorn tree. They chose one of the smallest trees as if they needed close family fellowship and were squawking and complaining as they competed for space. From bushes further down the track, we were being observed by a cautious *Vervet* monkey. Somewhere, his family were hidden. He was obviously the protective male.

"Granville, would you *seriously* think of coming back here?"

"I think about it *all* the time," he said. Bright with expectancy, he repeated, "*All* the time. I would come back tomorrow. And you, Annie, would you like to come back?"

"Well, I have spent the last few days chewing over the whole thing. There is a lot to consider…it's not simple." Before he could interrupt, I continued. "There are some wonderful changes in South

Africa where life is fairer for the indigenous people. Part of me would love to return and be a part of the growth and change, but I feel safe and comfortable in England—Africa still hurts me too much."

Granville nodded thoughtfully, and we walked on down the sandy path towards the shops.

9

My Hamster Wheel

In late July, we reluctantly climbed on the plane to return to England. It was not easy to say goodbye to Kate and Bill. We sat around drinking coffee for ages, only checking in at the last minute. Allan had bought so many curios for his friends and workmates and also to decorate his flat that we wondered how on earth he was going to fit his 'hand luggage' into the lockers. He was carrying his two tall wooden giraffes and lots of bulky paper bags!

Kate asked Allan questions that were on my mind at that very moment

"You seemed to have had a great time Allan. Did you think things have changed much since you were here in 1997? Do you want to come back? "

His answer was mature and thoughtful. He had noticed *huge* changes; some areas and villages were hardly recognisable to him. He felt good that there were now opportunities for the people who belonged in South Africa. He loved the smiles, the open-heartedness and the positive mindset.

"There is a unity amongst all the population, a willingness to make South Africa a great place, and a big welcome wherever you go."

He said that he valued being able to live in England where he could enjoy the art, the countryside and challenges. Nevertheless, his heart would always be in Africa.

"One day, I will be back. Here I feel I am on familiar ground. I understand and bond with the people. I feel connection to the country and close to Lucy with my memories of her. For now though, it is good to be going back to England. It's a kind of escape. I am not ready to come back here."

He had summed up how I felt too.

"Are you angry, Mom?" Allan asked when we were waiting to board the aircraft (Kate and Bill had left us to drive back to Pietermaritburg).

"Are you angry at what happened to Lucy? At leaving your big house, your friends and the business?"

How can I be angry? South Africa is now fairer than before. There are opportunities for the people who belong to Africa. There is more widespread justice for the native people, true owners of the land. And our time here was temporary. We, the whites, were the interlopers. I lived through the awfulness of apartheid.

I had always been embarrassed to have so much, and they (the blacks) had so little; there were many places and areas that they could not go. It is hard to believe it now (with complete absence of these regulation and thankfully few reminders), but the benches were labelled Whites Only *and* Non-White, *and so were the entrances to many shops, bottle-stores and the train stations. There were separate places for each race group. From a young age, I was shamed by the way the Africans were treated by the whites. I must have been seven or eight years old when the questions started: Mom, why can't Gladys eat at the table with us? Why can't she come to Church with us? Why does she have to sit on other benches? Why does she have to go to the back of the bus when she takes us to Durban? I cannot recall any of her answers, but I can remember thinking,* That's not fair. She's our friend.

As a young adult with my own home, I employed servants to help in the garden and the house, and I, like all other employers, had to register with Bantu Administration as an employer of blacks. Failure to follow procedure could result in imprisonment for both servant and employer, and searches were routinely carried out to check documentation. Each month, I had to sign the servants' 'dom pass' [employment records and identification book], which the employee had take to the Bantu Administration offices for the required official stamp. These frightening Gestapo-like institutions were usually presided over by Afrikaans men in safari suits. The shouts return to me like it was yesterday.

"Hey...Kaffir boy...your dom pass is not stamped! Go home (usually far away in a black homeland) and get it stamped by your Chief. Kan jy nie lees nie? [Can't you read?]" (No, he probably couldn't read. Blacks had to pay for their education; whites were educated free by the state). The fact that 'home' was 400 miles away and the poor chap had no means of getting there except by walking was totally lost on the brutal bastards.

I am back there in the old colonial house that served as their office. The floors are bare wood, and globe chairs are lined up around the perimeter of the room. The blacks, who file in one by one, walk across the floor to the far end of the room where the men in khaki sit. There is very little on the desks except for stamps, the inked stamp pad, and a few pens tied to the counter with cord. Behind the officials hangs a shombok [whip made of leather], and they are all armed with police-issue 9mm firearms.

I saw them strike out many times with a whip or a fist. The 'boys' came forward, fear in their eyes, sweat pouring down their faces.

"Shit...Kaffir, get back...off, don't crowd me."

Once when I intervened, the official turned his aggression towards me. It was verbal, but it was just as scary. I was told that I was a Kaffir-boetie (a person who loved the blacks as if they were brothers) and to keep my nose out of government business.

"*You watch out lady. I'll get you investigated! I've got your name and address. You could be in big trouble!*" *he spat out in Afrikaans.*

I am jolted back to the reality of now and Allan's question. I reply, "No, Allan, I really have no anger. I have no right to be angry. No right at all."

During the early part of the flight, I think back over the months of our sabbatical.

What a wonderful privilege it is to take time out. Granville has been happier than I have ever seen him. We've seen places and done things that were lifetime dreams. We've had time to think, calm down and restore our tattered souls. How fortunate to be able to come and go as we pleased. And for the first time since Lucy, Mom and Dad died, I've had the luxury of remembering and grieving.

"Thank You, God, thank You, Jesus," I said aloud.

Just before we tucked ourselves in with the pillows and blankets and as the plane was quietening down, I told Granville that I had been *seriously* thinking of leaving Global Real Estate. I said that I was not sure of what I was going to do and that I knew that it would be difficult to find a job at my age. I just felt that I could not go back to the situation at the office and the ever spinning hamster wheel over which I had absolutely no control. I had to move on.

I continued explaining. "The property industry is all encompassing; it kind of sucks you in. I know I am an achievement junkie, and I have a compulsion to do well, but I am dreading the thought of going back there. I have always said that if I lost the passion for a job, I would pull out. Now I have reached that point. In fact, I think I reached it months ago but didn't want to admit it, even to myself."

I think Granville had already sensed my misgivings, and for most of the remaining trip, he burbled on about the pending changes in our lives. 'What if this' and 'what if that'…and 'what if we could do this or that'…and if only he could get a job…'how are you going to cope without a serious job? It's your life'…and so on. I think I dozed off soon after leaving Johannesburg, but it was probably somewhere over the Sahara before Granville realised that I was sound asleep.

Within a few hours of arriving back at home, I got a call from the office that seemed a hundred miles away.

"We thought you were back! When will you be coming in to work? Tom wants you back as soon as possible."

Later in the afternoon, I called to see everyone at the Ascot office. The girls were delighted to see me, and I them. I had missed them (but not the work!) whilst we were away. We'd been more than workmates—we had become friends. I wished that each of my hardworking colleagues could have a long break like we had had. I gave them the little presents I had brought from South Africa.

"I'll be back at work at the end of July. Just give me time to unpack."

We were reunited with Pussy Willow that evening. She was glad to be back in her home. Although she had been lovingly looked after while we were away, she, like us, felt that it was good to be home. She settled back straight away—found her favourite spot on our bed and slept soundly until 5.30 a.m. the next morning. Rising dozily to feed her, I thought, *Only God knows how they got her to sleep later.*

Over the next few days, I knew with certainty that we had to make some serious decisions regarding the future. I was not sure that I could continue working at Global. Granville was determined to finish one of the books that he had started writing on the sabbatical, and I was sure that he had a good chance of getting a book published. After all, he has an extensive vocabulary and education, and the experiences he had survived during his life were amazing. I am still pushing him to complete the autobiography he started to write.

I am sure that if he publishes his life story, it will attract an enormous amount of attention. I am spellbound when he relates some of the incidents to me, especially the stories about the war from his perspective as a child. He has a particularly beautiful speaking voice, and I find that these reminiscences are not only part of his past but glimpses of history.

"Who wants to read about all the boring stuff I have been through?" he asked me when I was urging him to write his autobiography.

Then I told him I had nearly finished my diary about our year's sabbatical and intended to see whether I could find someone who would publish it. As first, he was a bit hesitant about it.

"Shouldn't you stick to what you know, Anne? And you *know* how to promote houses! If you want to write a book, fine, but don't let it distract you from your real estate work."

At the beginning of August, as I dressed for work, it came as no surprise that my business suits were *really* tight. Finally, I chose slacks and a blazer. With a feeling of 'first day at a new school', I sat at my desk working through the pile in my tray.

"Nice to see you in harness," said Loretta, the office manager, as she ran to answer the phone. Almost immediately, we were all occupied on phone calls or with clients that had come into the office.

By lunchtime, I was emotionally exhausted and thought as I walked to the supermarket to buy a salad, *I can't do this anymore.*

That evening, I told Granville that I was going to leave Global Real Estate. He asked me to try to clarify. I tried my best.

"Basically, I want my life back. I feel that it has not belonged to me for years! This time that I have spent away from the hectic business world has changed my attitude towards making a living. I would rather earn less money and have a life that was not exclusively work-driven—that will allow us to continue to have time for God, our friends, our family and for each other. I know that we can't duplicate our sabbatical; this has been a 'once in a lifetime' privilege, but in both England and South Africa before that, I gave far too much time and energy to my career, allowing it to control every part of my existence. I have spent long hours working or thinking about work; as an achievement junkie, I have been totally occupied in work-related matters—planning strategy on promotional projects and putting in those *extra long hours* to meet targets and deadlines. And much of this time was stolen from my family. Am I making any sense, Granville?"

"I am with you whatever you choose to do, Annie!"

He'd understood!

It took me more than a week after my return to work before I plucked up the courage to tell Tom Hegel that I was not coming back to work. He was quiet at first and then said, "The market is even quieter than it was before you left on your holiday, so everyone has to work harder. I understand how you feel. What are you going to do? Have you got another job?"

I was relieved that he took my resignation so calmly. I was expecting a drama.

"I have no idea of what I am going to do. We will do a whole lot more travelling around until next year. Then all I know is that I need to choose an occupation that will not demand my soul!"

"Well, that means you won't be back in *this* industry," he said laughing. "It has got to be the cruellest tyrant of the lot!"

I know I will miss the camaraderie, the challenge to excel for my boss, and the super office environments which were (and still are) the most modern and well presented in Berkshire and

Surrey. It's also been great security to know there was a 'pay-packet' at the end of each month. But having come to this final decision, I have an overwhelming sense of peace, so I know it's the right decision.

That evening Granville and I looked at our options:
- -Returning to South Africa.
- -Having me work in real estate here but in a less demanding role.
- -Opening our own property business.
- -Buying a house or flat to renovate then selling or letting it out.
- -Changing careers totally. (No suggestions forthcoming!)

ಌಌ

I left Global at the end of August, and until the end of the year, we took more trips in our camper in and around England and Scotland. It was getting much cooler, but we put on more layers of clothing and warm boots for walking out. We had great times; looking back at our photos the other evening, I commented that we had the most *fantastic* year of our lives. I felt immense relief that I had resigned from Global. I knew it was the right decision.

We had a super Christmas with the family; we both felt relaxed and invigorated. Granville did a full traditional Christmas dinner (with every trimming imaginable). I have no idea where he got all the energy—it took days of preparation. He adores the whole Christmas thing—our house and the tree were decorated (like the dinner) with every trimming imaginable!

After New Year, we continued on our travels. We took short tours by air and car to France, Germany, Switzerland, and Spain. Granville fortunately speaks several languages, always appreciated by natives of 'foreign' countries. He was so excellent at getting us up and running at short notice, each trip well planned and researched so that we saw and did as much as possible. We reluctantly returned home at the end of February and agreed that we should both put serious thought into our future. We continued to wait with unusually peaceful hearts for God to give us a clear directive.

On a freezing cold day in late March, we were drinking coffee in Starbucks, just off the high street of Guildford. A client (now a friend) walked up to our table to ask how we had enjoyed our holiday. We briefly shared some of our experiences with him.

"When will you be back at the office, Anne?" he asked. "I was just about to call in and see you at Global. I want you to help me to sell my house and find another one!"

I told him that I had left the company and was trying to decide what to do.

"Well, why don't you start your own business? We'll be your first clients. Do you want to help us find a new home and sell the huge pile in Virginia Water…the one *you* sold us in 1998? I *am* serious; I wouldn't want to go to anyone else."

My eyes widened, and in seconds I was mentally doing a business plan.

"Ja…okay!"

27th March 2004

Excuse me, I'm off to buy a couple of new suits (my others are really too tight), polish the shoes and dust off the briefcase. I'm back in business! Have I learned lessons from the past? Or will I let the business-animal consume me again? I promise—I'll let you know!

Printed in the United States
65445LVS00001B/502-549